2012
2023

MW00490115

2

3 24

The Postman of Abruzzo

THE FRENCH LIST

VÉNUS KHOURY-GHATA

The Postman of Abruzzo

Translated by Teresa Lavender Fagan

LONDON NEW YORK CALCUTTA

Seagull Books, 2023

First published in French as *Le facteur des Abruzzes*
by Vénus Khoury-Ghata
© Éditions Mercure de France, 2012

First published in English translation by Seagull Books, 2023
English translation © Teresa Lavender Fagan, 2023

ISBN 978 1 80309 152 5

British Library Cataloguing-in-Publication Data
A catalogue record for this book is available from the British Library

Typeset by Seagull Books, Calcutta, India
Printed and bound by WordsWorth India, New Delhi, India

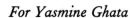

For Yasmine Ghata

'A village carved into the rock—it looks just like Eboli where Christ stopped, according to the film by Francesco Rosi, the last village after the last train station, the train can go no farther. Its name starts with the letter M.'

Luc's explanations were always vague, but since she was pretending to understand . . .

Her geneticist husband had forgotten the name of the village where his heart had broken down, even though he had been there 15 times and had brought back hundreds of samples, blood, urine and saliva, from its inhabitants—Albanians who had settled in Abruzzo over a century ago, all of the same blood group: O negative.

When he died following his return, his friends stepped over the piles of samples in the entryway of their apartment to offer their condolences.

Six cartons and a hundred pages of notes to decipher and rewrite—she always did it and would have done it again if Luc hadn't had the terrible idea to die.

Copying his notes was like accompanying him to those lands where he set out alone to meet the people he told her about upon his return: Eskimos in Newfoundland, salmon fishermen in

Alaska or the Albanians he would introduce her to during his next trip. At least, that's what he said.

There wasn't a next time. There would never be a next time.

The last of the consolers gone, and while waiting for Luc to no longer be dead and for him to come home, not a day went by that she didn't think of the Albanians of Abruzzo. After ten years and still no Luc, she took the train from the Gare de Lyon to Italy and to that village whose name began with the letter M. The file on the Albanians and her portable typewriter added to her suitcase at the last minute.

'I am the wife of the doctor who pricked the tip of your fingers and had you urinate in cups,' she would tell them, and they all would open their doors to her.

Those who have a view of the mountain watch her go from the train station to the house she had rented for a week. The others who have a view of the valley and who see nothing adopt the opinions of others, they have no reason not to. Her arrival at high noon in the month of August when the sun hammers nails into one's head doesn't surprise them, but they find it bizarre that she doesn't stop in front of the cemetery or the cafe, if only to drink a glass of water before continuing up the steep path.

'The last house on the left, below the ruins,' the woman at the rental agency had told her. 'And above all don't get lost, there's no one to help, since the inhabitants of Malaterra move to the valley during the summer. The mountain top is left to the vultures and the snakes.'

The key in her hand weighs a ton, as heavy as her legs as she attacks the steep path. The woman she has just left is gesturing wildly as if she were jumping rope.

'The key,' she shouts, 'is *pro forma*, the door doesn't have a lock any more, and you have to go down below to get supplies. Everything is down below.'

And she points to the valley.

'Is there a stationery shop?'

'*Porqué una papèteria?* The old people who knew how to write are all dead, the young have left. Unless you want to try your luck with the old Kosovar, he opens on Sunday after mass. What's your name?' she asks before walking away.

'Laure,' says Luc's wife over her shoulder without turning around.

The crushing heat slows her steps, slows her thoughts. She can't remember the exact reason that propelled her to this steep village and its inhabitants who speak a language that they alone can understand, a mixture of Italian and Albanian. Is it because it looks like Eboli, or to close the circle of her mourning that she travelled for an entire night?

Studying the genetics of men and women who live in a closed community, marry only amongst themselves and crossed the Adriatic to change their lives stopped Luc's heart. Samples taken during the day, analysed at night, notes written between wakefulness and sleep, deciphered and rewritten the next day.

Luc's writing is as torturous as the steep, arduous path.

The same houses carved out of the rocky mountainside, the same rusty facades. The sun and snow of Malaterra make the rocks bleed. They're caves more than houses with blind windows. The only open shutters are on the hastily rented house.

Lined up in front of the door are five soot-coloured kittens who seem to have been waiting for her to arrive. They lead her to their mother who is sprawled on the crochet bedspread. Madame mother who is recovering from giving birth yawns wide enough to dislocate her jaws, then follows with an anxious gaze the comings and goings of Laure between her open suitcase and the armoire where she puts away two dresses and Luc's folder of notes. Tomorrow she will read the pages in which are entangled in great disorder illnesses, immune deficiencies, inter-marriages or incest—the father impregnating his daughter with the mute collusion of the mother, sometimes the brother who has gone very far away and who no longer sends home news.

Tomorrow she will put some order into the geneticist's hastily written notes.

It has been ten years since he was evacuated to Rome in a blinding snowstorm, ten years since he returned to Paris in an ambulance plane transporting a half-dead man in a coma. Two ironed shirts sent a month later by a certain Helena still smelt like him. Touched, smelt, eyes shut tight out of fear that her tears would dissolve his sweat, the two shirts hanging in a closet swelled with the dead man's presence whenever the slightest gust of air reached them.

From her balcony hanging over the void, Laure makes out a steeple, a square, a tree with trimmed branches, and the red tiles of the roofs. The lake's evaporating water masks the houses, not the ravine, a gaping chasm, one of the seven doors of hell, says a railroad notice. Why had Luc chosen this village and its inhabitants to study? Did an entire population's common blood group merit so many years of research, staying with the locals, with his death at the end?

And who is this Helena who returned her husband's two shirts washed and ironed by her own hands? No address or phone number, only a sprig of bitter-smelling lavender included in the package.

A man is talking to the cats at the front door. He advises them to eat neatly and not to fight, otherwise Yussuf will get angry. He pushes open the door without knocking, isn't surprised to see Laure, quickly sits down on the only chair, wipes the sweat from his brow with the back of his sleeve before telling her, sadly, he doesn't have any mail for her, but he'll come back every morning nevertheless in any weather, even if no one writes to her or thinks of her, even if he doesn't know her name or where she comes from, to give the cats some milk—the mother has dried up.

A difficult birth, he explains in a tight voice. The poor mother almost died, the babies were breeched, Yussuf had blood up to his wrists.

His recommendation: don't move her from the bed.

Seeing the typewriter, he asks if she writes books and if she appears in newspapers and on TV.

'I'm just rewriting.'

'You mean you copy what someone else thought before you? Someone important, a minister or a president of the Republic? He threw his ideas down on pieces of paper, you correct the mistakes, unless the person in question is no longer with us, the dead can't reread what they wrote.'

Does he take her silence as an admission?

His hand on his heart, the postman offers her his condolences, his buttocks glued to the chair, the climb has exhausted him. He's going to get himself a glass of water from the tap before continuing his rounds in the valley, though his mail bag is empty. The young people don't send their news, they rarely return, only to bury a relative or in a casket. A fall from some scaffolding for some, a settling of scores for others. The Mafia recruits aggressively.

'The Albanians of Malaterra are scattered throughout Italy,' he laments, 'only your neighbour chose Australia. Deflowering Helena's daughter caused his house to crumble. The walls couldn't stand up after the poor girl's suicide, the same misfortune strikes stones and dishonoured girls . . . Do you know if Australia is in America?'

'Nearby,' Laure answers absently so not to lower herself in his esteem.

'To the right or the left?'

'A bit lower.'

'Or higher, since the earth turns.'

The postman clearly has the last word.

With one foot outside the door, he tells her delicately that she shouldn't expect him the next day. 'All of Malaterra will be at Sunday mass. The pews on the right reserved for the parents of the victims, the pews on the left for those of the killers. Blood feuds divide families.' He is the only one to have kept his distance from this barbaric practice imported from Albania. Rebibbia made him a civilized man.

Laure assumes Rebibbia is a woman, whereas the postman is talking about a prison. His two stints there:

'Three then six years, Rebibbia transformed me.'

He didn't kill as one might have thought, but had built a school that collapsed on the students. The only survivor was the teacher who was absent that day. His cow was giving birth. When he was released he didn't know how to do anything else other than put stones on top of stones, and so he started again and built a little wall that collapsed onto a goat, though he hadn't scrimped on the mortar. A recidivist, so twice as many years. He took advantage, learnt how to read. Back in Malaterra, the mayor offered him a mail bag with the promise of buying him a donkey, though a bicycle would be better given the descent.

Yussuf talks about the bicycle as if it were a woman. He calls the handlebars arms, the wheels legs, the saddle buttocks. She moans when you turn, cries with pleasure when she is ridden, sighs when you brake.

Despite his age, Postman Yussuf has a sensual memory whereas Laure's is aggressive.

'Who is Helena?'

'A woman who killed herself though she thought she was killing her daughter.'

'Is Helena beautiful?

'She is the least ugly of Malaterra.'

'Is Helena young?'

'She is the age of the bear of Abruzzo.'

The postman didn't close the door behind him, the house of the man who went to Australia appears in the doorway. One wall standing, scattered stones, and a tree in the middle of what must have been a bedroom. Bare, sickly, black branches. It looks like a broom standing upright on its handle.

That's where he raped the girl, the postman had said. Out of shame the tree eats its own fruit.

Laure watches the birds flying over the single wall. None of them land on it. In a hurry to return home, they slice the air with their razor-sharp wings.

She will eat the bread and thyme-filled cheese she bought near the train station even if she isn't hungry, sleep even if she's not tired, and push aside the cats nestled against their mother so she can slip into the bed.

The wind blowing up from the valley awakens her in the middle of the night, the door banging with a clap keeps her from falling back asleep. The wind of Abruzzo doesn't like foreigners, she says to herself, and she buries her head under the pillow.

Tomorrow she'll contact a locksmith.

Tomorrow she will rewrite Luc's notes on the Albanians of Abruzzo.

Postman Yussuf says he saw only once and from a distance the doctor who analysed the blood, urine and saliva of the Albanians of Malaterra. Having just recently been released from prison, he hadn't yet fully come to his senses. Gossips suspected the *medico* of planning to sell their blood to Parisians who were anaemic from squabbling over food, and of giving their children afflicted by whooping cough their urine to drink.

A doctor who was interested in fingerprints is certainly a police informant, said others.

'You had to piss three centimetres, not one less, into his little cups on which he stuck labels that he licked hungrily as if they were *chocolata*.'

Subject A, Subject B, Subject C, up to Z, then beginning again with A2, B2, C2, as if the people didn't have names or as if they were born out of the rock. Everything they did put into the *molineta*, the hopper. The *medico* wanted to know everything in order to calculate their *rythmo biologico* as he put it: whether they took a *siesta* or not, if they slept on their backs or their sides, if they made love standing up or lying down, in the dark or with the light on. Transported to Paris, probably dead, the *medico* con- √ tinues to be fodder for talk at evening gatherings. His name comes up in all conversations.

Laure's darkened face makes the postman feel bad. Less distracted he would have understood that she knew the *medico*.

'You must be his wife to have come so far,' he says awkwardly.

Postman Yussuf considers researchers' obsession with the Albanians of Abruzzo obscene.

They swoop in, ransack pantries, dig in the ground, in chicken coops, take notes, before disappearing forever. A doctor from Geneva convinced Yarmila to blindfold her chickens so they would lay twice as many eggs, and advised Milia to avoid pruning her rose bushes when she was menstruating.

'To talk about rose bushes and periods to an old woman who has neither . . . Only pebbles grow in the garden of Milia who has outlived all her children. Boys and girls died at birth. Once the mother delivered, the father immediately dug a hole in the garden. They named only those who lived a few days.'

What was the name of the one before? He had asked her.

Milia, who couldn't remember, scratched her head. The names of the dead babies vanished along with the blood of their births. Only children inscribed on the baptismal record have a name.

Sorrow dug a hole in Milia's head, no grass grows in her garden. Her children eat its roots. Yussuf is convinced of this while the absence of trees on the mountain in his opinion goes back to the first immigrants who killed each other for a bit of land, a piece of bread. The blood that flowed down the mountainside ruined the soil, ruined the rocky slope. What looks like rust is actually their blood.

Laure hears the bells summoning people to mass over the din of the bowls being knocked together by the hungry cats. Little pink tongues vigorously lap up the bread soaked in milk which the postman had brought.

Once down the incline, she reaches the esplanade where a crowd in black hurries along. One would think it is a burial, whereas the dead are further below, in the cemetery in the valley. Disapproving glances at her short skirt and uncovered head from the women. Watching her go towards the Kosovar's shop, young and old flock in front of the church entrance, their faces turned behind them. Whisperings and gossip blend with Gregorian chants.

The bookseller and stationer greets her with an effusive welcome. The lady from the agency told him she was coming, the postman informed him that she is writing a book on the Albanians of Abruzzo. He'll provide her the paper as well as the information she needs for her project which he calls *grandioso*. He knows the Albanians from every angle, inside and out, ignorant and arrogant, pretentious and illiterate, they have rarely crossed the threshold of his shop, they read coffee grounds and palms rather than the treasures displayed in his window.

'People of bowls and pots, not books,' he concludes bitterly.

12

Sweeping his arm widely, he shows her the mound of books covered in filth. All the dust of Abruzzo has come together in his window, but having cohabitated with it, he hardly notices.

A book loaned out along with the purchase of ten sheets of paper, he proposes, although Laure needs an entire pad.

Seeing her hesitation, he encourages her to accept.

'It's not every day that one falls upon Sophocles or Euripides published in ancient Greek. Plunge in your hand and take without looking, the heart sees better than the eyes.'

Dusted off with a great flourish but swollen with the humidity, the book Laure chooses weighs a lot. The title written in Cyrillic is incomprehensible to her, but not to him, he says he is amazed by her choice.

The book is the story of her life. Orpheus, who descended into hell to find his Eurydice, is her. He hands it to her. She'll pay for the ten sheets of paper. The book is a gift.

'Welcome to the hell of Malaterra,' he says sadly before ushering Laure to the exit. She would do well to get in front of the great heat, to go home without delay, the sun of the Christians kills. In a week she will show him what she has written. One page a day beginning with Helena. Her hatred for the Australian deserves an entire chapter. She has been waiting for him for 30 years, her rifle in her hand. The rusty barrel, her arms plagued with arthritis, won't prevent her from killing him, she will kill him a hundred times over. With the Australian dead, Helena will dance on his grave, then will sleep soundly. She will sleep for 30 days straight.

With Orpheus and the ten sheets of paper under her arm, Laure makes a detour to the bakery. The baker serves her the bread with a complimentary handful of olives, a gift from the house, and a warning against the Kosovar who judges the Albanians through his dirty glasses and his dirty shop window.

'He has never shaken our hands, never dipped his bread in our plates, never married one of our daughters. The only Muslim in Malaterra, in a word, a pagan. A worshipper of the devil, his Mohamed is only a messenger—just a messenger—he didn't create anything.'

Luc's notes are a magma of words and numbers. Only a scientist could decipher them. Laure is only Luc's wife, only his wife. Putting together the words he threw feverishly onto the pages, his eye glued to his microscope, would not make coherent sentences. She risks distorting his thoughts. She's not a writer, either, and has no interest in being one. Words obey only those who think them. With Luc gone, they have regained their freedom, have gone away, and it isn't the fingers of the one who washed and ironed his shirts that will be able to bring them back. How can she return meaning to the sentences he didn't say in front of her? For them to be said, she needs his lips and the vocabulary of a separate community that shares the same codes and the same secrets, revealing only the results that conform to its interests.

Creatine, variation, electrophoresis, steroids, ascorbic acids, genes, nuclei, cells, etc., etc.

The only word she understands: Malaterra, underlined in red.

His samples sent on to Paris, Luc prolonged his stays. Three days became six, twelve. Enclosed in sealed cartons, the blood and urine of the Albanians piled up in the entrance to their Paris apartment. Read and reread, all night long, his notes do not reflect the men and women she ran into in front of the church the day before. At daybreak Laure goes down the steep path. Her footsteps awaken the sleeping esplanade. The fire of the bakery, the only bit of colour in the grey early morning.

Why go out so early? And why did the cats follow her, meowing? The baker, who guesses their hunger, and hers, shares the last of a sausage with them and offers her a loaf of raisin bread along with his hand. He would marry her along with her cats, but as a second wife. He already has one. Irreproachable.

'Accept, and you will have bread at home, accept and you will have a woollen mattress, pots that shine like suns, and a window screen. The window screen is essential when all the shit of Malaterra is poured into the pond and the mosquitoes have stingers as long as a mattress maker's needle.'

The baker proposes marriage to every woman who enters his shop. His proposal made, he returns to his oven, his customers will arrive soon.

Men, women, children visible through the vapour of the sulphurous pond appear on the winding path in the valley where everyone has his patch of tomatoes, squash, eggplant for personal consumption.

Which one of them remembers the scientist who arrived on a day of blinding snow, a metal box in one hand, his suitcase in the other, and who went straight to city hall, the mayor having to accompany him on his tour of the houses, and who left the next day in another snowstorm without leaving an address or mentioning if he was going to return?

Subject A, Subject B, Subject C . . . up to the end of the alphabet. Luc should have used their names: Helena, Yussuf, to mention just those two. Designating them with a letter of the alphabet was the same as looking down on them. A disregard, a lack of respect. Subjects A, B, C up to Z—even after fifteen stays and three years digging into their genes and their blood.

The evening darkens the window and Luc's notes. An entire day without deciphering one page or rewriting a line. The Kosovar's ten sheets of paper remain untouched. Laure feels useless. Closing the folder, she falls into bed in her clothes without turning on the bedside lamp, without having dinner.

The postman's voice this morning is as heavy as his footsteps. Laure must excuse his absence the day before. His visiting rights to see his children take him to Cantanzaro every first Sunday of the month. His wife wants to maintain the ritual from his years in prison. Six hours back and forth on the train, and disappointment when he got there. The door locked. The children were inside. He heard them breathing. Heard their stifled laughter.

He called out all afternoon: Roberto, Raimondo, Renata. His voice lowered with the sun. Night fallen and he imagined them locked up in the darkness, he took pity on them and went back to the train station. Lights in the house suddenly turned on just as he walked away. The profile of his wife through a window was as lovely as that of the Virgin Mary.

'An *apparizione*.'

Postman Yussuf has only good memories of his wife and of prison. Without Alicia he wouldn't have had Renata, Raimondo and Roberto. Without Rebibbia, he wouldn't have learnt to read, and would have been illiterate like all the inhabitants of Malaterra.

'Read to escape,' the prison director kept saying. Those who took him literally were caught and put in solitary. He read.

Changing the subject, he asks Laure what the Kosovar might have told her during her visit.

'Mourad, who saw you afterwards, said you were black with filth.'

'Who's Mourad?'

'The kind baker, the Kosovar's whipping boy, the whipping boy of the rooster perched on a garbage bin who believes he's the friend of heroes because they're mentioned in his books. Ulysses, Alexander the Great, they're just dead men and entirely made-up people. Have never leaned over a kneader or baked bread, never blew on embers or relit a fire. The Kosovar, a big-mouth, a liar like the clouds that make you believe it's going to rain then disappear with the slightest wind. He must have told you that Helena wants to kill the Australian, though she just wants to make him pay the blood money for her poor daughter.'

'Because he killed her?'

Laure is horrified.

'Worse than killed, he deflowered her, broke through it like an eggshell, impossible to reclose her. Opened up as she was, no one would have married her had she had the misfortune to live. Her mother helped her depart.'

'Depart where?'

The postman's hand striking the air above his shoulder explains nothing.

His eyes sweep the walls, the floor, before stopping at Luc's folder.

He thinks that only the rich can blacken so much paper. They have time to waste.

Putting words on top of words doesn't construct a house, doesn't make a child or a tree grow, doesn't plough a field or prevent locusts from devouring an entire crop of corn. The pages one writes on a table don't change the shape of the table but make the brain of the one writing explode. Too many words crack one's skull and shorten one's life.

Postman Yussuf heats up as he talks. His tirade over, he explains to Laure that she hasn't come to Malaterra to read and write, but to meet people and share, without specifying what is to be shared—their happiness or their misfortunes.

He tells her about Rahil, who washes the dead and sends all she earns to her son who is making a fortune in Genoa but doesn't have time to tell her about it, of the forest ranger Ibrahim who found himself nose to nose with the bear and about his hair that became white overnight.

'It's as if it had snowed on his head.'

He also tells her about the anguish of Milia who no longer receives news from her husband who was washing windows in Milan and about the announcement of his death that has stayed in his bag.

Yussuf doesn't want to cause Milia any pain.

Milia is a widow, but doesn't know it yet.

The postman ends his account with the shrieking of Helena when she discovered the spot of blood on her daughter's dress.

Helena shrieked out of her head from one side of the mountain to the other, her shouts climbing the slope to the house of the rapist, dislodging stones, toppling over walls.

'Crushing the boy?' asks Laure, gasping.

The postman shakes his head.

They crumbled on themselves like a sick body. The rapist set off that very day for Australia. An Albanian cousin from the first immigration who made mirrors took him in before making him his heir.

Departing from Rome, he never returned. The tree that grew between the crumbled walls is perhaps his stricken body. Dead from shame.

✓ Why is the postman telling her about all these people she doesn't know? Laure understands every other word of what he is saying, speaking two languages at the same time, the words are Italian, the expressions come from elsewhere, and all the verbs are in the infinitive.

It would be better if he told her about Luc and his arrival in Malaterra in a snowstorm, a metal box in one hand, a suitcase in the other, without a coat, sure of being able to finish everything in a day: 12 hours to make an entire population urinate, bleed and spit.

'He must have grown to like it, to return again,' says the postman.

Thinking only of filling his syringes and his little cups and of writing things on labels that he licked hungrily as if they were *chocolata*. Our women didn't interest him. Did he have one in Paris? He never talked about it. Maybe he had forgotten that he was married.

✓ Postman Yussuf sends Laure to Helena who housed him.

'She can tell you better than I about the saliva scraped off the insides of cheeks, solutions of all colours, the Subjects A, B, C up to Z the way one recites the alphabet.'

Ten or fifteen stays, he was as healthy as a lion, and then there he was, stricken like he had fallen into a well. The thermometer exploded, Helena took care of him for his cough whereas the illness was in his heart. Useless the newspaper slipped under his shirt. He was suffocating. Useless the candle lit to the Virgin. The Virgin angry with Helena for the reasons you know wasn't going to listen to her. Seeing he was getting worse, the mayor took him in his jeep to Rome then handed him over to the airport doctor.

No news of him since then. Postman Yussuf has to believe he is dead since Laure says so, but he nonetheless warns her against her imagination.

'Rifling through the papers of a dead man isn't enough to bring him back to life,' he says perceptively.

His advice: pack them up and move into the valley. Living isolated surrounded by empty houses will end up ruining her health. Only the bear of the mountain endures, even if he howls his head off when the moon is full, as Helena did during the accursed night. The most accursed of all nights.

When Yussuf is gone, Laure opens Luc's folder, her fingers brushing the first line she sees without feeling the slightest vibration. The words have stuck to the page like the moss on his unattended grave. An image that turns her stomach. The one-syllable cry of a night bird calling out to her. *Luc . . . Luc* then silence. Between its two cries Laure waits for it to again let go of the name held in its beak, but nothing comes. Dissolved in the atmosphere, Luc buried in a crevasse in the air.

The sound of rocks tumbling outside awakens Laure in the middle of the night.

Footsteps approach her house, a weight pushes on the door as if to break it down. She thinks of the bear that howls madly on nights of the full moon.

'Get away from here, get away from here!'

Laure is the only one who hears her voice.

It won't be the spiny moustaches of the cats that will scare away the wild beast, or the chair up against the door. The bear of Abruzzo will swallow her and the cats in one mouthful.

Useless to call for help: she is alone on the mountain. Protected by the mountain side and the sound of the wind in their trees, the inhabitants of the valley can't hear her.

'Get away, you rotten beast,' but the mass of muscles and bones continues to shake the door.

Its breathing fills the bedroom. A humming motor, the sound of a forge, it breathes and sweats through the stones, slipping through the hole of the lock.

Continuing to shout risks exciting it rather than making it go away. Its growling comes from every direction. Laure is hallucinating: no walls to protect her, the door exists only in her imagination.

Did turning off the light disorient the bear? It growls angrily, gets up then moves away as the dawn begins to enter through the window.

Laure waits for it to be far enough to rush to the square and the bakery, the only shop open at this early hour.

She sobs against the baker's chest and tells him everything: the door, the bear, the growling, and how he will devour her when he returns.

Because he *will* return, her door doesn't have a lock, and she has only a screwdriver to defend herself, he will devour her and the chair, the table, and the crochet bedspread.

Instead of sympathizing with her fears the baker convulses with laughter.

The baker laughs and cries at the same time.

The image of a screwdriver trying to kill the bear makes him choke with laughter.

Nono, he says, is a vegetarian, eats only fruit and vegetables, never women, meat disgusts him. His back must have been itching, he wanted to scratch it and could only find your door. Nono is just a sack of fleas. No one has ever complained about him. He searches the garbage bins on winter nights when hunger ✓ chases him from the mountain, he's happy with whatever he can find, doesn't turn away from anything. Humble, discreet, knows he's a beggar, but feels no shame or vanity from it.

The conclusion: Nono is everyone's friend.

'Not mine.'

'A normal reaction. He will be your friend when he isn't afraid of you any more,' the baker proclaims lyrically, his moustache sagging with emotion.

As wide as dough kneaders, the baker's hands wander from her neck to her back, but Laure isn't offended. Arms that smell like wood fire, a chest that smells like warm flour. She is safe as long as Mourad is watching out for her. Mourad still wants to marry her.

'When I'm in your bed, the bear will beat it, he'll run away.'

When the darkness becomes even darker and the lights in the valley are turned off one by one, the bear doesn't return and Laure sleeps deeply and dreams of Luc for a long time. Wrapped up to his eyes in an emergency blanket like the ones passed out by firemen during fires, his voice reaches her fragmented, choppy. She retains one thing he said: over there, it snows all the time.

She must above all not tell him he's dead, the slightest allusion to that would make him disappear, and she wants to shout out how much she misses him. A missing as emptying as thirst and hunger, one that makes her mouth water, her nipples hard, turns her belly into a furnace.

When she awakes, she seeks the cool of the balcony. The valley seen from this height is a black bottomless hole. Leaning on the railing, Laure tries to imagine the sleep of the women sleeping below, women deprived of men. The mist of their breath covers the windows of the houses, the fetid odour of the pond clings to the skin of their dreams when they do dream.

The dreams of widows covered with black water. Liars who claim that their dead husbands glue their mouths to their windows, that they leave the imprint of their dark kisses there.

How can one believe them when everything is a lie around them? That it snows in the middle of summer, that what one thought was a pear tree sometimes bears apples, and that a cow gives birth to a half-man half-animal creature. Who is the father? Which male in Malaterra stuck his dagger into the gaping flesh of the beast? The priest threatens to cut off the member of the one who can't tell the difference between a rump and buttocks, between a silky pubis and a rough slit, and to throw it to the dogs. The priest who becomes heated promises other punishments, would list them willingly if the laughter of the flock didn't put an end to his exaltation.

Postman Yussuf brings Laure a lock—made of gold, he says, though it is really made of copper. Hammering and turning a screwdriver doesn't prevent him from making conversation. Informed of her misadventure, he explains that the bear Nono, whose real name is Valentino, is no more animal nor human than the inhabitants of Malaterra, but clearly more sensitive to the cold. On really cold nights, he gathers wood and makes a fire with two flints. His paws held over the flames, he rubs them with sighs of contentment which can be heard everywhere.

The postman's face lights up when Laure tells him about the baker's marriage proposal.

Yussuf sees nothing offensive about the proposal. There is nothing wrong with Mourad except that he spits into his hands before shaping the bread and he is already married and has five children. His snoring in bed would keep all the bears of Abruzzo away. As the baker's wife, Laure would have two *residencias*: a summer house in the valley for eating fresh greens and fruit picked right off the trees; a winter house on the mountainside where Mourad would warm her feet. And who knows whether he would give her children even if she is not a spring lamb. There remains the problem of his first wife and of the evil spells capable of thwarting his advances. But why worry about it? Everything in its time. Mourad in his Sunday best, a carnation in his lapel, is as handsome as the president of the Italian Republic, he adds. Generous, discreet, capable of giving half his coat to a beggar even if he has no coat and there is no beggar in Malaterra.

Responding that she will always be Luc's wife, even if he departed without warning, even if he didn't write and he forgot her, makes the postman uncomfortable.

He stares at his big, worn boots. His hand seeks something in his sack. Not finding what he is looking for, he suddenly empties the sack and picks up an envelope that has been folded so many times it is the size of a postage stamp, and he holds it out like a trophy.

'It's for you, and remember—I had my reasons not to mail it. The *medico* went back to Paris half-dead. He would tell his wife what was in the letter if he recovered. In the opposite case . . .'

'In the opposite case?' Laure repeats in a choked voice.

'I would have given you back the cost of the stamp. Yussuf isn't a thief.'

The two lire that he takes out of his pocket fall on the ground. He doesn't have the strength to pick them up.

Her lips pressed together so not to explode in anger, Laure asks him if he has other letters like this in his sack. She accuses him of withholding information, of appropriating someone else's property, of theft, and Yussuf, who can't understand how one can put oneself in such a state for a few hastily scribbled sentences, compares Luc's writing to ants. He even talks about itching and scratching one's heart until it bleeds as Nono did on the door. If he knew how to write, he would have recopied the letter a hundred times, to be pardoned. But Yussuf only knows ✓ how to read.

My love,

Everything reminds me of you when I'm with these people who don't know you, are nothing like you, don't speak the same language as you.

They are as alone on their mountain as you are in your large apartment.

Violent wind in Paris all week long, according to yesterday's newspaper.

You must have fought against the windows that don't shut well and plugged up the gaps with paper. Some wood is like people, it grows stubborn with age. Cold-blooded as I know you to be, you must seek refuge in bed as soon as the sun lowers behind the chestnut trees.

Your knees up to your chin, your head resting on your shoulder, you sleep with your face turned to the door.

How can I tell you without humiliating myself that these images bring tears to my eyes.

My poor love, will you pardon me one day for not having had the time to love you?

I'm writing you this letter to help you remember us.

Luc

A love letter from Luc, splinters in Laure's heart, warm rain on an overheated land, doesn't cool her, doesn't quench her thirst for him.

A single hand can't applaud, and the same is true of letters written by the dead.

Does Luc love me more since he died? She wonders, forgetting that he wrote the letter while he was alive.

She reads it over and over for three days, from top to bottom, and from bottom to top beginning with the last sentence until the words become dizzying and nauseating.

Piled on top of each other, the words don't recreate a man, don't rebuild a dwelling. The dead Luc has taken the dwelling with him.

Empty rooms, an empty bed. No one called. She no longer went out, saw no one. The streets, the passers-by were hostile to her. She slept, she got up.

The only event: the day.

A visit to his grave, never repeated, concluding that with both of them dead it was as much his duty to visit her.

At that visit, having arrived with empty hands, she had taken a wilted bouquet from a neighbouring grave and had tossed it onto his with the feeling of a duty accomplished. She offered flowers to the one who had never given her any. His first name engraved on the stone linking to the one that ended the strange letter.

Smoothing out the crumpled page doesn't erase the folds, nor the wrinkles on her face made deeper by sleepless nights.

Born to live alone. The five kittens, loaned out for the duration of her stay in Malaterra, as Luc was for her life as a wife, will not fill her life.

His tenancy having reached its end, Luc was taken from her. The geneticist departed without his microscope or his test tubes, without his indecipherable notes on the Albanians of Abruzzo. Would returning to the place where they were written make them more legible? As enigmatic as his writing, dead Luc retains all his mystery.

After returning from a trip to China to study throat cancer related to the consumption of fish salted and dried in the sun, and seeing the toll taken on his wife's face, he had suggested to her to take advantage of his absences to have fun and make new friends. 'A boyfriend,' he had specified, half-serious.

Shouting at him that he was her only boyfriend had exasperated him.

A complete change the next day, taking back his suggestion, he said that he had expressed himself poorly and that he wouldn't be able to live with the slightest lapse on her part. She would wait for him as long as there was blood in her veins and a door that would open at each of his returns.

Luc's letter, a musical instrument that emitted no sound.

A useless object, incapable of knocking down the wall that is separating them.

Her ear glued to the paper, Laure doesn't hear his voice, nor the sound of his heart when he had written it. The paper doesn't retain the smell of his skin, doesn't retain any breathing. Made out of a tree, it dies like everything that moves: people, rivers, seasons.

Postman Yussuf won't cross the threshold until Laure has pardoned him. He is there for the cats he calls Raimondo, Renata and Roberto—the names of his children—to feed them and to chit chat with them.

Used to his quirkiness, the cats pay no attention to him and jump on the food.

Yussuf doesn't understand their mistress' anger. Such drama for a letter that he would have ended up sending one day. Ten years in his bag without throwing it out shows his good intentions. His heart told him that he would hand it over in person one day. Postman Yussuf doesn't trust the mail.

Ten winters and as many summers, without his protection that letter would have fallen out of his bag, would have landed in Mourad's oven or between the paws of the bear.

The postman would have sent it to Laure if he had known her at the time.

As a matter of principle, the postman only holds onto the letters of people he doesn't know.

He sees things differently now that he sees Laure as she is: not single, not married, not really young, not really old, with a bear that scratches its back on her door, and above all missing from the city-hall registers.

Imagining her dead, she perplexes everyone. In which tomb should she be buried? Whom should be notified and to whom would the gravedigger's bill be sent?

The shoemaker who saw her in the distance says she doesn't fit into any mould, skinny as she is. Yussuf feels responsible for her since he experienced the face of her anger.

Now that he has emptied his heart, he stands up. He will continue on his rounds. His footsteps fade away on the steep path that he climbs every morning for her, only for her.

'But what could have attracted Luc to this lost corner of the world?' Laure wonders and she closes the shutters again, plunging the bedroom into darkness, though the day has just begun.

The two bureaucrats from city hall wearing suits, ties and hats want to question Laure about the report her dead husband wrote on the inhabitants of Malaterra.

'People above all suspicion, the crème de la crème,' says one.

'Salt of the earth,' adds the other.

There are still grey areas surrounding this project sponsored by the former mayor, a Communist from the Stalin era. A corrupt man, they both agree.

Calling a report mere scientific analyses amounts to turning Luc into a police informant, a snitch, a spy.

Laure hands them the folder, then retreats to the open door with the cats.

They arrived in the morning, and when the clock on the square rings noon they still haven't put their hands on the slightest disparaging or suspicious text that would discredit the inhabitants of Malaterra. Subject A, Subject B, Subject C, up to Z are not necessarily Helena, Yarmila, Mourad and the others. Not even the slightest allusion to the Kosovar, or the postman, or even the mayor, who played an important role in this matter.

Disappointed and above all aware they have wasted their time, they straighten their ties, close the folder stained with the

sweat of their brows after concluding that the report written in
French, a verbose language, is of no interest. It would have been
different if it had been written in Albanian, poorer in vocabulary
but clearly richer in meaning.

They leave Laure, stepping backwards, hands together with
respect as if she were the pope or the king of Siam.

Outside the door, they ask her if she has inherited her dead
husband's work tools. Microscope, stethoscope, test tubes, syringes and needles would be welcome, they would buy them
half-price. Malaterra lacks everything.

The Kosovar wants to read the ten pages he sold to Laure two weeks ago, whereas she has written nothing and has no intention of writing.

'I am not a writer. I am a widow.'

'So you are a seamstress. Their husbands buried, the women of Malaterra buy a sewing machine and pedal to forget their sorrow.'

Laure says she doesn't know how to sew, either.

✓ 'Then you cook, your status as a female demands it. Granted, the cow doesn't cook, but she gives her milk.'

'I stopped cooking when my husband stopped eating,' she says, sure to move him.

But the stubborn old man insists on demonstrating to her that nothing prevents the dead from eating.

'They eat the smell of bread, drink the mist of the springs, burp, fart. Burps and farts go around in circles in the water of the lakes and the ponds.'

The tear that escapes from Laure's eye makes him feel bad. He would like to console her but doesn't know how. He has only one piece of advice to give her: leave the dead man to make his /

life as he intends, and above all don't harass him: 'Masses, candles, and prayers put the dead in a bad mood.'

When his left eye starts to sparkle, Laure knows he has an idea.

The Kosovar puffs up like a rooster ready to crow and suggests she manage his shop without receiving a salary since she will inherit it when he dies.

Offer settled. You begin tomorrow. You'll have to take everything out, power wash the walls, the floor, the window, his old man's armchair, his jacket, his sarouel trousers, and why not his poor handicapped body—his last bath was years ago—then dry everything before arranging the books in alphabetical order even if they're not written in the same alphabet.

✓   'Pride of place to Greek, since everything comes from that,' he insists, 'and because the world would be inhabited by donkeys and pigs without Sophocles, Euripides and Socrates. May Allah in his goodness receive them in his vast paradise.'

Laure will not manage the Kosovar's shop, nor will she marry
the baker, nor will she become best friends with the bear of the
mountain, but she will meet Helena who had seen the death of ✓
Luc in her coffee cup the day his heart gave out, according to the
postman.

'Did she really see it?'

'Just as I see you and you see me.'

'What did the death look like?'

'Something black, devious, and determined. Armed with a
giant fork, maybe a scythe, it whirled it around and plunged it
right into your poor husband. Swirling the grounds and beginning again didn't change a thing. The same threatening figure
came back with the same fork. All she could do was break the
cup. She did so without regret, without considering the cost. The
French *medico* was her son on the left side of her heart. To live a
stone's throw from Helena without visiting her was to insult her,
as an elder, a widow, and an orphan she has the right to respect.'

'Orphan?' Laure asks.

' . . . of her daughter.'

The postman's tone allows no response.

Even the mountain mourned the girl, only the mother's eyes were dry. She cried inside. Condolences poured in from every direction: plastic buckets of every colour, aluminium pans, wicker baskets, even a nightingale in a cage, but nothing consoled her. The priest who refused to give absolution because of suicide was immediately replaced by another priest. No people are more solidary than Albanians. It makes sense! The same blood flows in their veins . . .

. . . And the same blood type, said Luc, that of the Tatars who travelled the steppes of Asia, pillaged, raped, burned everything they encountered until the day when, either fatigued or because there was nothing left to pillage or to burn and no more girls to rape, they settled in a land squeezed between Greece and Yugoslavia before the Ottoman Empire and Communism scattered them just about everywhere on the planet—in America, in Australia, and mainly in Italian Abruzzo—children and fowl crammed into the same bundle, and prohibited from marrying foreigners so not to break the chain of blood.

'The blood of a virgin is her banner and that of a murderer a bargaining chip. Everything is bought and sold with blood,' explains postman Yussuf.

The blood debt, the blood tax, an Albanian invention.

A blood group and type common to all, but different DNA and chromosomes. Luc attached great importance to the chromosomes that vary from one individual to another. The skin scraping taken from inside a cheek is a signature. Only true twins are an exception to the rule. Chromosomes can reveal pathologies or illnesses likely to strike an individual during his life, he insisted, enable one to know if he will develop cancer, a cardiovascular illness, or other anomalies.

'Whether he will be an honest man or a criminal, a genius or an idiot,' Laure had added, falsely naive.

Her jokes didn't make the scientist laugh. His wife was as wild as the cells that multiplied without reason under his microscope. If it had been seen through that microscope, would life have appeared more enthralling to him?

He hadn't cried out, nor been horrified after the loss of the child she was carrying, but clenched his fists before seeking refuge in his lab. Three days and three nights walled up in his silence, without answering her calls. He wasn't punishing her, but was consoling himself in the company of cells.

The postman listens to Laure talk about cells, chromosomes, and genes without agreeing with her, without disagreeing with her, even when she reduces him to a scraping of his cheek, but doesn't seem to agree with all the rest.

His verdict falls like an axe:

'Instead of wasting his time with cells, the *medico* would have done better to spend more time with his wife, taking her to the movies or sharing a pizza in a *trattoria* instead of messing around with people's urine and blood. Poking, making people spit and piss lengthened the lives of the others and shortened his. He must be kicking himself wherever he is. Regrets are useless when you can't ever take something back. The past, says a proverb, doesn't console the present. A broken life can't be put back together, can't be glued. One can do nothing with it except look at the pieces and be sorry.'

Yussuf plans to give Laure a gift to make her feel better. He asks her to choose between a goat, an umbrella, or a walk in the valley to meet Helena.

'To meet someone worse off than you makes the sadness more bearable.'

A saying for every situation, all arguments work to distance Laure from Luc's folder which she drags around like a ball and chain.

✓ She didn't come to Malaterra to recopy her husband's notes, but to bury them where they had been written.

✓ Luc's writing became his only imprint on the world following the loss of his child. Back home after three days of silence, was he going to tell her he was leaving her?

His key in the lock pierced Laure's heart, dug a hole in it. The door opened, Luc picked her up, spun her in the air, covered her with kisses. His absence had been beneficial. He discovered that prisoners and chickens raised in cages have the same level of serotonin due to the same depressive state.

✓ Luc's research—his true life. Laure had to make do with his shell, clothe it, feed it. Shirts put on, meals eaten quickly, he went away, always away. The researcher devoured the man a bit more ✓ each day.

The same sounds rise up from the valley every evening. The shouting of women, the crying of children, the beating of the wings of birds frightened by the sudden darkness, the whipping of sheets chasing off coyotes, reach Laure's ears in bits and pieces.

Tomorrow she'll follow the postman to the houses hidden between two rock faces.

Tomorrow she will meet the women with faces hidden in coloured scarves seen in front of the church.

Shouting, cries, beating of wings become a din in her head and send her back to her solitude when the lights suddenly go out. An entire community bonded by the same habits and schedules like the stones of a building, whereas she is only a pebble that rolls with the wind.

Tomorrow, Laure will put a face on the one who sent her Luc's shirts after seeing his death in her coffee grounds.

43

The one who for 30 years has been waiting with a gun for her daughter's rapist greets Laure with ululations. It isn't every day that the wife of the French *medico* honours her with a visit. Her hand cupped like a bullhorn in front of her mouth, Helena calls to her neighbours who in turn call to their neighbours. They pour in from every direction, dishevelled, wearing slippers or barefoot, make her sit on the only armchair, cushions under her elbows, feet on a stool, before in a single voice requesting news of their blood.

'Did the doctor look at it carefully? And what unpleasant things did he see? Which one of us will live to be a hundred? Which will die young? Who will become rich and who poor? Will Helena meet her daughter one day, and in which heaven? Are the promises made to men accessible to women who have suffered?'

Do they confuse blood with coffee grounds?

Laure explains to them that blood doesn't hold images, blood is like a river, it is the soul of ancestors that flows in our veins.

Heads nod in understanding.

Half-convinced, they go on to Luc whom they call Luka.

Does he still have his long needle that jabs the arms on either side? Does he still like Maria's pickles and Fila's stuffed peppers? And does he still talk with his pipe between his teeth?

✓ Pretending not to know about his death is a matter of politeness, only Laure is entitled to tell them about it.

She accomplishes this with a smile so not to spoil their day.

But they appear to have been stricken by lightning. Their faces darken, they moan, wail, throw themselves on her, pat her hands, rub her back, give her handkerchiefs whereas they are the only ones crying.

Is distress obligatory in this type of situation?

They talk about Luc at the same time, nodding their heads sadly, mention him between laughter and tears: he liked to drink raki, smoked the hookah, played backgammon with the men, cheated.

✓ Are they talking about the same man?

Laure's austere Luc was quite drab compared to theirs who loved to eat, joke around, was cheerful, never tired.

✓ Worthy descendants of rhapsodists, each one has an anecdote to tell. Their rare encounters with Luc filled their lives while a cohabitation of ten years with her fit into a handkerchief.

✓ Whether their memories were true or made up, Laure decides to hang onto them.

You have to forget everything to bring back memories, and she asks the question that is burning her lips.

'Did Luc talk about me?'

Of course, is the collective response. But it's better to ask the girls, mothers have sieves for brains.

Almost as old as their mothers, the daughters make great efforts to remember what Luc said without betraying him.

'The *medico*'s wife spent her days battling dust,' says one.

'Battling germs,' says her neighbour.

'Battling noise, shutters and windows closed during the day,' cries a third, waving her arms around.

They judge Laure according to their own criteria, make things up, sure that Luc is unable to contradict them:

'Incapable of preparing a hookah, his wife.'

'... or of wringing the neck of a chicken and plucking it.'

'Passed out at the sight of blood.'

'Has never eaten fruit right off the tree.'

'Can't tell the difference between a loaf of bread baked in an oven and one baked between two stones.'

The most serious allegation kept for the end:

'Drinks bottled water, is afraid of the fountain and the well.'

'Luka's wife, a madwoman,' cries a deaf woman who doesn't know who Laure is.

Antigona followed the movement when she saw the others running to Helena's house.

'Tell Antigona to be quiet,' could be heard coming from all directions.

Antigona muzzled, they console Laure with the warm cloths of affectionate words though she refuses all consolation. Consoling herself means forgetting Luc, dismissing love.

Constantly moving, exhausting, they want to keep her for lunch and why not for dinner and to spend the night in the valley, there are plenty of houses and mattresses. She can leave tomorrow after the morning coffee and grounds reading, Mariam reads them like an open book even though she never went to school.

Laure promises to return, to have lunch with some, dinner with others. She needs to go back to her house, she is tired, very tired. She has to feed the cats.

Sympathizing looks. The sterile woman who considers the furry bastards her children incites pity.

She stands up and they stand up. She thanks them and they feel obliged to thank her. Kisses smack on cheeks, she's eager to escape the arms that hug her, the hands that rifle through her bag to make sure she hasn't forgotten anything. The packages piled up at the door are meant for her—produce from their orchards. She'll think of them when she makes imam bayildi, does she want the recipe?

She'd really like a fig from Helena's fig tree.

Faces and mouths shut, fingers point to a photo taped to the mirror. A girl who is neither pretty nor ugly, but luminous, stares at Laure with her pale eyes.

The face of Helena's daughter, a spot of pain and incomprehension on a polished surface.

Having arrived in a great brouhaha, Laure leaves them in a great silence.

'What was Helena's daughter's name?'

'The dead have no name,' grumbles Yussuf, walking in front of her on the path.

The postman considers the girl's death less important than her shame. To have arrived deflowered on her wedding night would have been the worst of humiliations.

He reproaches Laure for having complimented the fig tree. To ask for the fruit of the tree where her daughter hanged herself must have wrenched the mother's heart. No one picks them, no one eats them, the fruit is left to the birds.

Guilt crushes Laure's shoulders. The bags of vegetables at the bottom of her arms are suddenly very heavy. She sets them down. Let Yussuf make *bayilidi* out of them. She will not eat vegetables that grew around the grave of the dead girl.

Their paths split at the square, Laure allows her tears to flow now that his back is turned. She cries for Luc and the girl who no longer has a name, cries while walking, continues to walk even though she has passed her door. An urgent need to see up close the house where the girl was raped and why not the bear, a habitue of the place, with the hope that he will attack her and she will shriek at him the way Helena had shrieked that accursed night. Tempt danger, die. Anything but the silence that fills her from inside.

Laure's visit to Helena causes a stir in the valley. The women who patted her, loaded her with sweets and gave her vegetables from their gardens consider it bizarre. It's impossible to classify her in a known category.

She's not widow enough since she travels alone and isn't wearing black for her husband.

She isn't single enough for them to find her a husband.

Nor is she a woman of ill repute for them to chase away with stones after breaking one or two of her feet.

Laure is only like herself: a woman who does nothing with her ten fingers except eat and wash herself.

The women of the valley rack their brains to find an occupation for her that would make her a woman they could be around.

It's unthinkable that they would confer the instruction of their children to her, she doesn't know their alphabet.

She doesn't have a green thumb, the geranium on her balcony has died from not being watered.

She doesn't have the makings of a cook since she gave their vegetables to Yussuf who couldn't keep his mouth shut.

Nor does she know how to sew, her unravelling hem and the button missing from her blouse didn't escape their notice.

The women of the valley went over all the professions, all the occupations, and found nothing that suited Laure.

Above all she mustn't work in a hair salon with the way she looks—hair as straight as string beans without the slightest wave or ringlet to draw the eye of a man. Some even wonder if she can read and write, given the work that awaits her since her arrival which she puts off day after day.

An entire folder on the inhabitants of Malaterra, according to the rumour, as thick as a wool mattress. They are all in it as God created them: blood, urine, as formidable as a camera.

Having observed her well when she was drinking their coffee, the women from the valley said nothing at the time and kept their thoughts for later.

Arms too thin to pull a bucket up from the well or a cow from a pen, too weak to catch a chicken, cut its head off, plunge it into boiling water and pluck out its feathers. No heart, either. Her kisses on their cheeks, a chicken pecking pebbles.

They would willingly look the other way from her short-comings if she had inherited the healing gifts of her husband.

Conclusion: the *medico*'s wife lacks character and above all courage to have dampened Mourad's apron with her tears because a poor bear scratched its back on her door. As harmless as a baby chick, Nono, all witnesses say so. Hibernates half the year. No one knows where he rests his big body. Vegetarian, Nono wouldn't hurt a fly.

The women of the valley above all reproach her for her lack of social graces. To arrive empty handed at the home of a lonely woman is unheard of. She could have picked a pear or an apple on her way. Even a nettle would have done.

A woman who twiddles her thumbs all day long is like a cracked jar, a pot with a hole, a coffee pot without a handle, a rusty basin. They don't hold anything, are of no use to anyone.

'Only Ruhié had good things to say about you,' concludes Yussuf the following day.

'Who's Ruhié?'

The old woman dressed like a whore. Her daughter who earns a living sweating at what cannot be mentioned gives Ruhié her old dresses which she wears for their smell. Yarmila works from an apartment in a storefront right in the heart of Napoli. She gets married every day, but never with the same man, boasts Ruhié who considers virginity old-fashioned, her daughter got rid of hers at the earliest opportunity.

She must have missed her mother to have arrived, two years ago, in a car filled with presents.

An unexpected welcome, she left that very evening, her face bloody, a broken wrist, her dress torn, and her car dented everywhere. The women welcomed it with stones. The children jumped on the hood and sang at the top of their lungs:

Yarmila *putana*.

Ricca *putana*.

Morta *putana*.

Seeking refuge in the station while waiting for a train, Ruhié's daughter didn't attend the distribution of her gifts. She hadn't left out one of her mother's neighbours. Having become a perch for chickens, her car is rusting in a vacant lot. Ruhié continues to frequent her daughter's tormenters but doesn't say anything to them. Her silence and Yarmila's dresses on her old scrawny body, worse than an accusation. A condemnation.

Postman Yussuf does not have a clear conscience, he told Laure half of Helena's tragedy but kept the other half to himself. The girl had no desire to die. She would have still been alive, mocking the sun with her pale eyes, if her mother hadn't hanged her. The girl's cries filled the valley, hammered against the walls of the mountain, fell back down on the head of the mother who had become her executioner. She begged her to pardon her, kissed her hands, kissed her feet, promised not to do it again, to never lie down beneath the boy, to never again trust a man.

Having become as deaf as her well, Helena had dragged her daughter to the fig tree then tied the rope around her neck before kicking over the chair. The true guilty one having left for Australia, she turned her rage onto her daughter. Someone had to pay.

Her task completed, Helena emitted a ululation that roused all the inhabitants of the valley. The first to arrive didn't see blood, but a sparkling whiteness hanging from the tree. It looked like crystal or a flow of frozen water. Pushed aside those who wanted to take her down, only her mother had the right to touch her. She laid her on the edge of the well, then washed her the way one washes a baby, in every fold. When she reached the pubis, she scrubbed furiously at the drop of frozen blood that looked like a ruby.

No shroud, no casket for the dishonoured girl, but a newly ironed sheet, the daughter in the arms of her mother as light as a dress, as a basket to collect grass. Helena thought she was carrying a dead girl, but she was really carrying two. She was deader than her daughter.

The girl buried in a hole in her garden, the mother slept face down on the turned-over earth to better hear her daughter breathe.

Three doves were waiting for her at her door when she awoke. Their sharp song was an accusation: Hohohohohoho repeated endlessly with a final questioning 'ho' though she had no response.

'Shut up, you dirty creatures.'

Helena shouted at them before picking up her rifle and shooting.

'Pan pan pan.' The shredded feathers flew in the air before resting on the well. From that day forward its water tasted like blood.

Helena would clean the well once she has killed the rapist.

She has been waiting for him for 30 years, since the devil in short trousers played marbles. Yussuf has counted well. The man's letter to the mayor announces his return. It has been sitting in his bag for three days. He's waiting for the seventh day to give it to him. Wasn't he told to turn his tongue in his mouth seven times before speaking? But that was in times past, when he was a child.

'Before Rebibbia.'

Laure asks Yussuf if Helena knows about the Australian's return.

'She knew about it before the letter, from the cracks that appeared around the little grave. Useless to fill them up, they returned as soon as her back was turned. It's as if her daughter wanted to come out to give her version of the facts. Thirty years underground chewing the dark in silence, she has had all the time she needs to grow and reflect. Her account risks weighing heavily if her mother allows her to speak and if she agrees to listen to her. But only stones don't listen, stones don't have ears.'

The excessive heat and the shame of holding onto the mayor's letter turn the postman's face red.

When he got out of prison, Yussuf swore he would become exemplary. His postman's bag on his shoulder and his cap on his head, he makes his rounds even if he doesn't have any mail to deliver. The exhausting climbs, feeding homeless cats or being otherwise useful are his punishment. He is atoning for the death of the students, of the goat. The goat, he says, returns in all his dreams. Its desperate bleating makes him wake up in a cold sweat. He even wrote a poem to it in his head since he can't write. You will be the first to hear it.

A hand on his heart, the other pointed towards the ceiling, Postman Yussuf recites in a voice brimming with sobs:

As light as an almond flower in the spring breeze
As white as rain in the desert
Your life shorter than lightning
La tua vita, la tua vita.

Postman Yussuf's hand falls down at the end of the poem.

Feeding hungry cats, protecting mad people, and helping Helena avenge her daughter is his way of atoning for his sins.

Seeing the fear on Laure's face, he explains that only Helena's hands will kill, not her heart.

'Helena, who took him for a drum, beat on him so badly that he no longer makes a sound.'

Laure feels less like a widow since her visit to Helena. The women of the valley who know his tastes and remember all his conversations are Luc's real widows. They're the ones who should wear black. The more they talked about him the further from her Luc seemed. His features became blurred behind their words. Her husband henceforth belongs to those who fed him and made him laugh. To Helena who housed him, washed and ironed his laundry, to Ruhié who brought him börek and stuffed peppers, Albanian dishes for the man who claimed to be a descendant of a line of Albanian nobility banished from the land by the Communist Enver Hoxha.

'*Medico arnaout,*' boldly declared the old Antigona, disturbing Laure.

'What is *arnaout*?'

'*Albanese,*' was the response given by ten mouths at the same time.

Albanian—the one she had always considered French, who had grown up in France, and who was hired by the French SACLAY, the temple of scientific research.

'*Arnaout,*' such an ugly term, once applied to the Albanian mercenaries enlisted in the Ottoman army. Laure rejected it despite the photo of the house in Gjirokaster. Lined up in front of the imposing structure, the entire family: three girls on the right of the parents, the only son on the left. The father with a monocle and a square-cut goatee, a low bun and pearl necklace for the tiny mother who just reached his armpit. Everyone was smiling at the camera except the son who was staring at a point outside the photo, a sardonic smile on his lips.

'Selim Bey, Fakhria *hanum* and their children,' written on the back.

A photo that escaped a country cut off from the world for three-quarters of a century. King Zog kicked off the throne and Albania became a bastion of Communism, the son who in the meantime had been named consul in Skopje found himself without a job and without identification papers.

'Forget us. You will be hanged if you step foot in Albania,' the man with the monocle had written to him in a letter conferred to an apostolic nuncio, the last one to leave Tirana. 'Take a boat to Istanbul and go see my friend Nessib Bey in Beylerbeyi on my behalf. His house opposite the pier is the highest on the east bank. Marry one of his daughters, he'll find you a position worthy of your ancestors and your qualifications. Director of the National Library, Nessib Bey is an influential man.'

His passport now useless, the next day the man who would become Luc's father rang the doorbell of the rich notable. The three-story dwelling exuded wealth. Velvet drapes on the windows, rugs from the Caucasus on the floors, valuable objects in glass cabinets. When the father clapped his hands two young girls emerged from the growing darkness. The eldest, a tall, graceless girl, held out a freezing hand while the younger smiled at him warmly. 'Rikkat and Myra,' announced the father. Disgrace and grace, thought the visitor, and his heart leapt in his chest. The last consul of King Zog proposed marriage the next day. Myra had stolen his heart.

'Rikkat must be married first,' the father declared firmly.

Married at the beginning of November while the Bosporus beat furiously on the pilings of the house, Rikkat became pregnant and was alone two weeks later. Having left to look for work in Geneva where he had gone to school, the husband who had nothing but scorn for the East reappeared after the birth of his son. What happened during the week spent under the same roof as his wife for him to have left again, but with the baby in his arms?

After 30 years away from his mother, Luc didn't know what she looked like. In rare photos, her face had been cut out. A hole on top of a dress, shoes and thin legs holding up a thick body. Entrusted to a nurse then to the Jesuits, the priests became his true family. Did his mistrust of married life go back to that period? Working in a team but living alone and never in a lasting relationship until he met Laure who came to one of his lectures. Married and living in his home where he would return between two conferences, Laure was often alone. A little Luc on her hips would have made her feel less abandoned.

✓ Did Luc have a child with a woman in Malaterra? she wonders for the first time, and an icy shiver runs through her. Tomorrow, Sunday, when mass lets out, she will study the faces down to the bones looking for Luc's features in all the ten-year-old children. A little Luka with a face chiselled by the sun of Abruzzo more useful to the memory of Luc than all his studies never picked up by other researchers. Their faded ink made them illegible.

'A baker's floury hands are just as good as a postman's covered in blood.'

A master of the art of alternating between hot and cold, Mourad says he has nothing against Yussuf except his marriage to a girl of another race, an Italian. With a Genovese woman on his arm, he walked around like a peacock, spoke only Italian, the words he lacked replaced with gestures. He took himself for a dictionary then for a *costruttore* until the day his school fell on the students' heads.

The poor guy thought he would get away with it by paying the blood tax. With his money in his pocket, his lawyer screwed him instead of defending him. Years and years in prison. After the fifth, Yussuf didn't count any more. Back in the village, he wandered like a madman, hallucinated. Having learnt that the fingernails of the dead continue to grow underground, he saw those of the children who had died because of him pierce through the dirt, reaching up to scratch him. The scratch marks he showed were stigmata. Both assassin and saint. The Kosovar called him Dante. Made sense, he had returned from hell. The poor guy would have begged in front of the church if the mayor hadn't given him the job of delivering the mail that was as sparse as the hair of an old man. Those who leave don't write, those

√from here don't trust a piece of paper, the heat softens it, the snow erases the writing. Long ago was the time when one could dictate a letter to the Kosovar. Having become old and ornery, he mixes two languages in a single sentence. In addition, out of rage his ink well dried up, say the gossips.

Laure returns the *Orpheus* the Kosovar had loaned her during her previous visit.

He asks if the book helped her find her husband the way Orpheus found Eurydice.

Has he forgotten that she doesn't read Greek?

One need not read a book, he says, to know its story. Legends circulate better in the open air, they travel on voices, from mouth to mouth, from country to country. Legends don't need an alphabet to exist. You must look at the pages the way you look at a beloved person, follow the lines with your finger without trying to decipher the writing. Like a pet animal, a book needs to be tamed. You must breathe it in, touch it, caress it along the grain to know it.

Unaware of how he is hurting Laure, he accuses her of not having the desire to find her husband again, otherwise she would have read *Orpheus*, even if it were written in Aramean or Sanskrit. Unless . . .

'Unless . . . ?' Laure repeats, on edge.

' . . . you doubt he's really dead. His body buried, you suspect he's returned to Malaterra to find God knows who, which explains your presence in this village of mad people and your

63

visit to Helena to pull information from her whereas Helena no
longer talks ever since her hands hanged her daughter from her
fig tree. As mute as the wood of her rifle, as the edge of her well,
she will talk after she kills then will mourn in huge sobs
of words.'

The bookshop owner doesn't hide his disappointment. He
thought Laure was of a different stripe. Alas! She's no better than
her two friends the postman and the baker, no better than the
Albanians of Malaterra, the amnesiacs who have forgotten their
language. Nomads who wander in their own heads.

   Dipping their bread in the same dish doesn't make a
community, a native of Tirana is nothing like a native of
Peshkopi. The Communist Enver Hoxha after the Ottoman Ali
Pasha of Tepelena scattered them to the four corners of the globe.
They scampered off like rabbits. Those with long legs pushed
on to Kosovo or farther to America, those with shorter legs or
Arvanites stopped in Greece and Abruzzo. Enhanced rumours
reached them. Ali Pasha of Tepelena sold healthy Albanians off
as slaves at the Messina market, cut off the heads of the old and
those who couldn't work, soldiers raped the girls, made women
pregnant. Blood flowed in the streets and houses. Enver Hoxha,
50 years later, closed the borders. The country shrunk like a wool
shawl washed in boiling water, retreated into itself, became a
prison.

   Why is the Kosovar telling her all these horrible things? Ali
Pasha of Tepelena and Enver Hoxha are not among Laure's pre-
occupations, they didn't kill her ancestors. Luc's genetic studies

are her only connection to the Albanians. And it isn't the scattered memories entirely fabricated by the women of the valley that will make her one of them.

For these women, she's the foreigner. Even the Kosovar considers her as such. He has just wished her a good journey back to her country whereas she hasn't yet decided the date of her departure.

Seeing her at a loss, he asks her not to misinterpret his intentions, he would be happy to keep her in Malaterra if it were his decision. Didn't he propose that she manage what he calls his bookstore without spending a single lira? Bookstore owner! An honourable profession reserved for the educated and for knowledgeable people, he stressed.

Did Laure's refusal hurt him? His eyes glinting, he claims that Ismaël is not vindictive, is not angry, is not mean. Only ignorance and stupidity make Ismaël crazy. The Creator has put hundreds of alphabets at the disposal of humans, those who have learnt to read and write will go to paradise, the others to hell where devils with giant pincers feed the fire with the books they didn't read.

'*Basta*,' he says, and his hand strikes the air above his shoulder.

He wants to be alone. Laure understands this when he turns his face to the wall.

The package tied with a string is his good-bye gift. Laure will read it far from his eyes.

The package from the Kosovar contains a parchment. Upright in the middle of the road Laure reads this:

> When it is time for you to die you say:
> Darkness only frightens the night
> And the frightened dead need only stay at home
> Holding their black breath.

What do these lines have to do with her.

Surrounded by rocky walls, she continues walking. Not a single tree or bird on her path, the Albanians of Abruzzo live six months of the year in dry and arid conditions, and six months in the earth and humidity.

She has made her decision: tomorrow she will pack her bags, give the key back to the agent. Tomorrow she will take the train back to Paris.

From the Kosovar's long speech she has retained only his first name: Ismaël.

Laure should have kept the Kosovar's words to herself instead of sharing them unfiltered with the postman.

Yussuf says he's outraged. Unacceptable that a Kosovar, thus a born Communist, with no ancestors or descendants, and Muslim to top it off, would criticize people bonded like the fingers on your hand under the pretext that they borrow words from their Italian neighbours. The inhabitants of Malaterra navigate between two languages like pigeons between drops of rain, without getting wet or catching a cold. Yussuf is more than outraged. He says he's offended.

'This isn't the Kosovar's first attempt at defamation.' Two years ago, he took the opportunity after mass to invite us into his shop. He wanted to show us something. After we went in, he immediately lined us up in two rows: the shorter people in front, the taller ones behind, like in school, really squeezed together, no one dared move or cough.

Standing in front of us all, he took out a pencil and said the word pencil, syllable by syllable, as if we were seeing a pencil for the first time in our lives.

Thinking it was a game, the short and the tall repeated 'pencil.'

He did the same thing with an eraser, a pencil case, his glasses, and finally with his worn slippers which he waved above our heads. Without thinking twice, the two rows took off their shoes and threw them at his dirty head. Their humiliation avenged, they went home and enjoyed their lunch.

First and final lesson. From that day, no one has gone into his shop. The result, he stopped cleaning up, stopped buying and selling. His shop having become a trash bin, people hold their noses when they walk by. Worse than a trash bin, a grave, his books written in dead languages. We're just waiting for him to die to turn it into bonfire and dance around the flames. But the wretch doesn't seem to be in a hurry. Takes on the years in reverse, the more he has, the more he loses. No one here knows how old he really is. No one can count beyond 100. The idea of making him pass over to the other side in a creative way has become an obsession. Someone, it doesn't matter who, proposed strangling him, someone else would claim the crime, and everyone in Malaterra would pay for the funeral.

They wouldn't skimp: flowers, candles, Gregorian chants—even though he's Muslim—even women mourners will pretend. Once the Kosovar is put in a hole, then the funerary meal: stuffed sheep so the dead man can graze the grass of the other world, mountains of pastries to sweeten his passage into hell, and enough ouzo to drown his soul which can't swim. During that time, another person who is neither the strangler nor the one organizing the funeral will clean everything. Hosing down, black soap, bleach, the trash bin transformed into a jewel, into an ARTISAN STUDIO, pronounced ARTISANA by the postman Yussuf who plans to have Laure manage it.

'You'll sell all the products from the valley: eucalyptus for those who cough, senna for the constipated, hellebore for the mad, cannabis for the overexcited, and for the chilly, wool gloves, scarves and sweaters knitted by our women, the bear Nono, the logo of Malaterra, in the middle of the chest.

'You'll keep the profits,' insists Yussuf, the only person who wants her to stay in Malaterra.

Helena thinks only of piercing the heart of the one who deflowered her daughter, cutting off what he has between his legs and throwing it to the dogs. Once the rapist is buried, she will finally be able to enjoy her fig tree, eat figs until she bursts, and make jam with the rest which she will sell to the tourists who, in October, flock to the strange village where even the poorest have two houses and the uneducated speak two languages. Extraordinary.

'All the inhabitants of Malaterra are worth the detour,' proclaims the mayor. 'As solid as Roman statues, standing as straight as Greek jars, whereas everything around them is falling into ruin: the mountain is eroding, the river is flowing underground, rain and snow transform the ravine into a lake and the esplanade into a skating rink. Malaterra is hibernating, so is its bear.'

Return to the valley after the thaw. The ice that cracks tinkles like animals' bells. People sweep, dry out, replant. Helena finds her daughter through her fig tree, the arms of the dead girl swing in the branches, her saliva gives its honey to the fruit. Ruhié once again puts on her daughter's enticing dresses, and Milia, a widow without knowing it, continues to wait for her husband. The others, all the others, dry herbs on their roofs, can their vegetables, and knit warm things for the next winter. All the women of Malaterra are widows, even those whose husbands are still alive.

Living below is as exhausting as living above, says Yussuf, but none of them complain.

Everything having to do with Helena's daughter upsets Laure, though she doesn't even know her name, nor the sound of her voice. It's her face, neither beautiful nor ugly, but phosphorescent from its pallor that keeps her in Malaterra. She will go back home after the denouement. After the Australian arrives she will leave without looking back, without explanations, without goodbyes, nor promises to return. Her shutters closed, the key returned to the agency, they will understand that she is no longer there. Weighed down by his bag, Postman Yussuf will not be able to catch up with her. Anchored to his oven, Mourad will not lift a finger to dissuade her. The Kosovar nailed to his armchair will watch her go away. The Kosovar sleeps, eats, shits in his shop for fear of being burgled.

A thousand and one reasons compel Laure to leave Malaterra and its inhabitants.

The only lure: the landscape which she finds different each time she looks at it. The ravine this evening is a land of stones, snakes, and black corn that grows all by itself, unharvested, its closeness to what they call one of the seven doors of hell makes it food for the devil. Higher up, a stone's throw from the valley, the church, its doors swollen by the humidity, its windows darkened by the smoke of the candles, the church never visited by

Laure who is angry with a God who took her husband from her. The Kosovar, the church's next-door neighbour, says that the ceiling is covered with bats who beat their wings frantically causing a deafening din as soon as the priest takes the host out of the tabernacle. The ceiling dripping with their guano, they feel at home, and perform their circus acts, hanging above the heads of the believers who never stop watching them.

No! Nothing connects Laure to the inhabitants of Malaterra. They think she's skinny compared to their fat, round women, miserly because her dresses don't go below her knees, a heretic because she has never set foot in their church even for the annual ceremony of the assault when, closed up for 23 hours without eating or drinking, adults and children chase the devil away with the same gesture, their mouths whispering the same sound: *pst, pst, pst . . .*

She can't stand all that they love: the bear, imam bayildi, senna, cannabis, and the blood tax. Even her blood type is the opposite of theirs: A positive, whereas they are all O negative.

Does Luc's death compel her presence among them?

Arriving in her dreams yesterday out of the blue, without knocking on the door, without even greeting her, he rummaged in her purse, in her suitcase, under the mattress, even in her pockets without providing any explanation. Luc, she finally understood, was looking for the key to Helena's fig tree to free her daughter from the tree bark. He was getting angry, swore he had left it in this room whereas he lived in the valley while he was staying in Malaterra. Luc knew he was lying, it was clear from his gaze that avoided her while his hands continued to search. His face suddenly lit up when he saw his folder.

'We're saved, we're saved,' he repeated twice. Having come without his glasses, he asked Laure to find the pages on the tree's DNA, the same as that of the daughter, he specified. 'The Australian arrives tomorrow. Time is of the essence. Helena needs proof to kill him. I alone can provide it.'

He pressed Laure to find the pages, the page, though she had only one desire: touch his hand, touch the wedding ring identical to her own that encircled his ring finger.

Had he guessed her thoughts? Luc pulled his hand away when Laure approached it.

The same attempts and the same frustrations as when he was alive. It is her destiny never to grasp him.

Awake and with her eyes wide open, Laure continues her dream and rifles through the folder, without conviction, knowing that it is impossible for a human being and a plant to have the same DNA and the same genes.

The mountain across from her is black. It goes up, descends. The mountain breathes. It has the worried profile of Luc when he was turning the pages.

Having entered her dreams freely, she sees his visit as a reproach. She shouldn't have followed him to Malaterra, should have rewritten his notes instead of wasting her time with useless discussions with the postman, the baker, the Kosovar. Should have washed his tall body instead of conferring that task to the morgue employee who had the grotesque idea of dyeing his

beautiful grey hair raven black. Should have visited his grave
more often and would have perhaps brought him back to life by
telling him of his recent return from Malaterra while not
reminding him that he was dead. Dead and buried in a Parisian
cemetery though he said he was Albanian. But he didn't—nor
did she—want to believe it. The imposing house in Gjirokaster,
the man with the monocle and his wife in her Sunday best, the
son a former consul of Albania in Skopje, the stateless man, the
reluctant husband of an unloved woman, a fiction, a fable, Laure
had trouble accepting it. It took the visit to Helena and the word
'arnaout' shouted by every mouth at the same time for her to
accept it.

The night air breathed in, in large gulps, at the railing of the
balcony calms the rapid beating of her heart. Helena's house, the
only one lighted in the valley. The obligatory light to illuminate
her daughter's path if she ever has the desire to return. The
words of the postman to be taken lightly but which Laure in her
turmoil never doubts.

Going back to bed, her footsteps resonate strangely on the tiled
floor. Only her face cries on the pillow. She, herself, doesn't cry.
Hasn't cried for ten years although she is always cold even in the
middle of August, in Malaterra where even the mountain
suffocates from the heat.

A red car cannot drive by unnoticed in such a chalky landscape. It follows the labyrinthine road without touching its edge, without darting off the cliff. Laure watches it until it reaches the foot of the embankment where it comes to a stop in a cloud of dust. The opened doors expel two figures: a man and a strange half-adult half-child creature. Maybe a dwarf. The rectangular object tied to the baggage holder, then removed with great care, is a mirror.

Why a mirror when there is only the sky to reflect?

A mirror, a dwarf, and a man stock still in front of a ruin.

What he sees is not a house but a pile of crumbled stones.

Tomorrow, when the news will have made the rounds in the village, some will say they heard him cry, when he didn't cry, nor did he lament. His distress is expressed by his great pallor.

Massive agitation in the valley. Dishevelled women run from house to house. Children and birds fly around in all directions. Everyone saw the car, the dwarf, and the man standing in front of his dismantled house.

Laure calls him a man, whereas those who watch him from the valley, their hands shielding their eyes, call him the boy, the Australian. A boy disguised as a middle-aged man: greying hair,

74

white suit. Only the car is red. The colour of the blood of the
rape of the girl who was neither beautiful nor ugly but luminous
who, according to her mother, has been demanding what is owed
her for the 30 years she has been underground. All of Malaterra
supports Helena. Laure is the only one who doesn't. To pay for
a rupture with coins will not bring her daughter out of the hole.

The mirror leaning on the only standing wall is an eccen-
tricity, a slap to those who don't have one, the Australian's
obvious desire to frequent only his own image. His letter to the
mayor announcing his intention to create a mirror factory to
provide work for the unemployed has remained in the postman's
bag. No one defends him. The enemy of all. He should have
waited for Helena's death to return. To return to a house
abandoned decades ago is to tempt the devil. A ruin rather than
a house. Houses whose soul is tied to the stones crumble when
their master stops looking at them. The years knock around in
his head. He left the village one autumn evening, the linden trees
in the valley were yellow, a fine layer of snow, the first of the
season, crunched under his feet, the good-bye wave of his mother
who begged him not to delay, remained in the air like a wing
pulled from a bird.

'Don't turn around,' she cried out to him. 'And don't even
think of returning. I'll let you know when I'm dead.'

The name and address of the Albanian cousin slipped into
his pocket at the last minute reassured him. A seven-letter name:
Mikhaël, followed by Durres, the name of the village of his birth
in Albania. To find Mikhaël de Durres, owner of a mirror factory
in the jungle, ten kilometres from Sydney, was harder than
finding a needle in a haystack.

The Malaterra forsaken at the end of autumn rediscovered at the beginning of September is not the same. Nor is his childhood home. A cantankerous grass has grown between the walls. Thistles, thorns, needles, as far as the eye can see. Stones that were once yellow are now white, the scattered bones of the skeleton of a dead house.

He talks to Laure on the other side of her doorway, in English, as if he knows that she isn't from here.

He needs water, lots of water to drink and to wash up. His friend and he have driven all night long, took the longest way, got lost, Malaterra appears on no map.

No! They don't need bread or eggs or coffee, only water. They'll go shopping tomorrow.

'Is there a market in Malaterra?'

She says there's a baker and a bookseller.

He knows about the bookseller, who was there back in his time, but not the baker. The women made their own bread.

His pail filled to the brim, he apologizes for bothering her. He will return tomorrow with flowers to thank her.

Need she remind him that the earth of Malaterra produces only what is useful and strictly necessary—vegetables—flowers left to those who live in the city?

Visible in the waning light, his strange companion jumps around like a rooster, from stone to stone, photographing everything he sees, click clack, click clack, even the clouds that are becoming blacker and blacker. It will rain tonight. The usual September rain. Nothing to fear, they have a tent. They thought of everything, even a folding table opened with a twist of the wrist by the pseudo-photographer, two chairs, and on the starched tablecloth a silver candelabra with five arms. The wind causes the flames to dance. Standing behind his master's seat, a spotless napkin over his arm, the majordomo offers a dish, serves, takes away the empty dirty plate, replaces it with a full clean one of beautiful porcelain, watches the candles, relights the one that has blown out. Out of a record player set on a stone surges the pleas of Bellini's *La Sonnambula*.

> Ah! Non credea mirarti
> Si presto estinto, o fiore,
> Passasti al par d'amore
> Che un giorno solo duro.

The singer's voice strikes Laure right in the middle of her chest. *La Sonnambula*, Luc's favourite opera. He listened to it over and over when he was depressed.

Laure sees the record player, the man, the servant and the candelabra in the mirror. Refined movements by the man who eats, mechanical movements of the one attentive to his slightest needs. They talk together while Laure remains mute in the mirror.

The singer stops singing and the meal is over, a first drop of rain falls on the man's forehead, his eyes study the sky then the houses with closed shutters before stopping at Laure's, the only ones open. He stands up and goes into the tent, the back seat of the car left to his servant.

The rain, the first since the beginning of the summer, starts falling shortly after midnight. Laure thinks of the one who is sleeping in his tent and her heart clinches so tightly that she almost can't breathe.

The morning finds her back at her window. The man and his servant have disappeared. Did she sleep so soundly that she didn't hear the car driving off?

Only the mirror is proof of their presence yesterday, otherwise she would have thought she had been hallucinating. A vulture appears in a corner, furious and committed he pursues a family of swallows, breaks the symmetry of their flight, sows disorder. Which among them will be his prey?

Helena bursts into Laure's house and accuses her of protecting the one who ruined her life.

'You gave him drink and food, you sang to accompany his dinner.' She kept hearing: '*Addio, addio mio amore.*'

Laure is so flabbergasted that she allows the woman to continue when she starts searching around the room looking for clues. The same frenzied movements as Luc's looking for the key to the fig tree.

Is she looking for the Australian under Laure's bed? Not finding him, she kneels on the ground and bursts into tears. Laure, who doesn't know how to console her, lies. She swears she saw her daughter in a dream. Radiant with happiness. She gave her a message for her mother. She asks her to pardon the Australian and to eat all the figs from her tree, leaving the rotten ones for the birds. Surrounded by maternal fig trees, where she is now, she needs nothing else.

With her index finger on her temple, Helena thinks. Her voice reaches Laure from a distance, as if from the bottom of a well:

'I don't know if your dream is a dream or if you knit it with your own hands which know only how to write words forwards and backwards. But I would have to be born from the same hole as the bear to believe you. Do you have another dream to sell me?' she shouts before slamming the door behind her.

Another enemy, Laure says to herself sadly.

Farewell, the promised curtains, sewn on the sewing machine carried on donkey or the postman's back. Farewell, any provisions for winter if she ever wanted to prolong her stay in Malaterra.

Helena had been counting on Laure's window to watch her daughter's rapist, to aim her gun at him. It was from her window that the bullet would fly.

A talented tactician, Helena had foreseen everything and had explained her plan in the smallest detail.

Laure would invite the Australian to share a hookah. A pinch of cannabis in the tobacco, 'you pass the pipe back and forth while discussing this and that. A puff for him, a puff for you, he won't hear when the shot is fired.'

'What if the bullet hits me?'

'Impossible, if you don't move.'

Seeing Laure hesitate, she yelled at her.

'Are you my friend or not! Did you eat my cucumbers and stuffed tomatoes or not? Do you sympathize with my sorrow or not?'

'Sympathizing doesn't mean killing,' Laure ventured.

The wrong thing to say.

'Who's talking about killing?' Helena has never intended to kill. She simply wants to talk equal-to-equal with the man, put an end to a misunderstanding that has lasted too long, the fact that he'll be sitting across from her makes the discussion easier. Alternatively, if Helena misses her target, the bullet will go into the wall.

Laure tells Postman Yussuf about Helena's visit, about Helena's anger.

But he doesn't believe her. A painful whitlow prevents Helena from going out. She feels diminished and shuts herself up at home. Will only go out to kill. When she'll be able to pull the trigger.

Laure is speechless with horror.

Does he take her silence for agreement?

He becomes bolder and asks her if she intends to marry the Australian so Yussuf can give the key back to the agency.

What has she done to make him foresee that outcome?

Water, he says in an imperative tone. You shouldn't have given him any. You begin by giving water, then your heart.

Laure's laugh humiliates him. Might as well call him crazy, he was just concerned about her future.

Is she going to move in with the Australian or not, so Yussuf can decide what to do with the key?

He reminds her *pro forma* that what the Australian calls his house is only a tent without any conveniences whereas here she is enjoying a tap and a toilet seat.

Laure has been warned. She should no longer count on him if she ever moves. 'Let the other guy feed the cats.'

Changing the subject, asking after his children does not make him less prickly.

It's better to talk about beautiful things, he replies. My children are ugly, uglier than a toad, a rhinoceros, and a gibbon.

Postman Yussuf is quite surly today. The reason for his distress is there, he says. And his fist beats his chest hard. He is homesick.

For where?

Rebibbia is the response, said as if it were obvious.

Yussuf, a freed slave who misses his years of slavery.

What would Luc have done in her place? What decision would he have made? Helping Helena amounts to being complicit in a murder.

Having become what he became, Luc is incapable of advising her. Luc, a blackboard from which everything has been erased. His bones have not retained Subjects A, B, C, haven't retained their blood group and type, nor their DNA. None of his collaborators resumed his analyses. No scientist studied his samples. Only he was interested in the Albanians who had fled the Ottomans then the Soviet regime of Enver Hoxha to settle on a mountain in Abruzzo. His passion for these people exasperated Laure. The cartons marked 'Malaterra' sent to the laboratory the day after his burial, never opened again, their contents expired and Luc's notes as indecipherable as Helena, Yussuf, Ismaël, and Mourad. Seen from her balcony, they are as tiny as letters of the alphabet.

With nightfall, they disappear in the margins.

Old fashioned, racist, prisoners of their customs and their blood that they cause to flow at the slightest disagreement. Their eyes highlighted with kohl are seductive. The hand armed with a dagger kills. The blood debt is in their genes.

Postman Yussuf tells Laure about Rozafa who sold her sheep and rooster to buy a revolver and a train ticket to Milan to kill the blond woman seen on her foreman husband's arm. Rozafa served five years in prison, but she shares her husband with no one.

Strange that Luc didn't detect the crime seed in the DNA of Rozafa or that of vengeance in that of Helena. The blood of the Albanians of Abruzzo, rich in pride. No tolerance for the one who walks on your pride or tramples your dignity. Only blood erases the affront.

During his many stays in Malaterra, Luc must have used extraordinary diplomacy never to have offended them. Six cartons of sensitivity, embitterment, tensions, and hatreds filled the entrance to their Paris apartment. So many trips for such a short life. Maybe he is in China or Alaska when she thinks he is dead. Maybe he's waiting for her in Paris and he has turned their home upside down to find his precious folder. She has to go home. Luc needs her help, she alone can give him back his notes; the denouement of the rape committed three decades ago must absolutely not keep her in Malaterra.

She tells the postman that the Australian and the dwarf have left.

He responds that they will return, because only rivers don't flow backwards.

She tells the baker that the Australian and the dwarf have disappeared. He responds that the one she calls the Australian is a child of the land and the dwarf a man like any other and that being short doesn't prevent him from having feelings.

She tells the Kosovar that the son of the land and the short man have left the village, he responds that they will reappear one day or another, as they left the essential behind them: the mirror, every inhabitant of Malaterra will see him or herself in it in his or her reality. Helena as a murderous mother, Yussuf as a happy prisoner, the baker as Hades, god of Hells due to his struggles with fire.

What about the others? All the others?

Pebbles that roll down the slope. The pebble retains nothing from its route, doesn't know it's a pebble. They are ignorant! Have never read a book. Read coffee grounds and palms. Don't know who Ulysses is. For them Homer is a fisherman on the Aegean Sea.

And me?

84

Laure's question makes the old bookseller pause.

A wanderer between two worlds. Half-underground, and half-aboveground. Who knows which of the two is more dead. An abandoned woman, he adds with the intention to wound, clings to gossip, rumours and superstitions to fill her void. Came to Malaterra to kill time, would kill it with a rifle if she had one, unless Helena loans her hers. But Helena's rifle has only one bullet, intended for you-know-who. Undoubtedly it no longer works.

With his tirade over, the Kosovar tells her that the mayor tried to reason with Helena who listened to him without interrupting before declaring that she would not kill the Australian before collecting the blood debt owed for her daughter. He is thus benefiting from a reprieve.

'A leech, she wants the bear and the bear's skin, which is contrary to the *bissa*.'

Says the Kosovar.

'What's a *bissa*?'

The price of a life, a manhunt, a race against death between the family of the victim and the murderer who has an interest in paying the blood tax to the guardian of the tower before he is caught. Having settled his debt, he will be able to look them in the eye, even to taunt them.

Practised far from Albania, the *bissa* has lost all its flair, the postman laments. There is no tower in Malaterra, no one to catch, this new generation can't run. People argue like fishwives, they pay, they spit three times in their hand before pocketing the money and patting the killer on the shoulder. No winner or loser, even if it means beginning again at the slightest disagreement.

The great writer Ismail Kadare tells of this pursuit in *Broken April*. A man attempts to outrun his pursuers. He hears their footsteps behind him, their breath on his neck. The tower is within his sight, will he reach it and pay the tax that will clear him before he is killed? Laure, who has forgotten the end, calls upon Yussuf's memory. But Yussuf has never heard of Ismail Kadare, nor of *Broken April*, Yussuf has read only two books: *Colonel Chabert* and *Crime and Punishment*.

'At Rebibbia we read only Dostoevsky and Balzac.'

He knows *Colonel Chabert* by heart, the man who had the same misfortunes as the Australian. Back home after being gone for years, no one recognized him. Chased away like a dog by his wife and his servants.

Laure learns from the same source that the mayor advised the Australian to stay away long enough for Helena to die a natural death, but he refused. He had waited long enough. The stones that fell from his house will ultimately crumble. The shrunken photo stained with oil dug out of his wallet shows four exterior walls and twice as many inside. The openings suggest eight windows and a door. He wants to rebuild the same house, within the same landscape. His memory has retained a mountain, a valley, a ravine, but erased the girl who died because of him, as he has been told.

Did he really rape her? What was her name? Where did she live? The Australian has forgotten everything. He doesn't deny the accusation, nor does he confirm it. He asks only to understand why 30 years ago his mother who loved him so much pushed him into a train to Rome where he set off that same night for Australia. An Australia no bigger than the palm of a hand, and a stone's throw from Albania, when seen on a map. He expected a crossing lasting a few hours. Thirty days living between the sea and the sky. Perhaps the boat had veered off course, the captain's compass had broken. Passengers and crew condemned to travel around the oceans until the end of time. The fear of wandering forever made him nauseous. Crouched in a corner of the bridge, he vomited bile, vomited images of his childhood, vomited Malaterra and his mother whose death a year later had no effect on him. Why were they so solicitous in telling him about the death of that woman? It was a new man, without memories and without a past, who was taken in by the rich Albanian who offered room and board to all his compatriots then hired them at his mirror factory. Albanian traditions dictated it.

The Australian compared the ruin to the photo as Laure did Luc's notes to the Albanians. The creatine, catecholamines, and hydroxycorticosteroids that represent Yussuf, Mourad, Ismaël, Helena, and all the others, do not make the first a good postman, the second a baker who doesn't spit in his hands, the third a true bookseller, and the last a tolerant woman. Helena wants the deed and its opposite: to kill and to collect the blood tax.

'It is not because the dog has four legs that he can run on two paths at the same time,' says Yussuf, sighing.

He feels sorry for the mayor who is attempting to diffuse the situation.

It is true that your house has collapsed, he says to the Australian, but tell yourself that it still has the same view. No one has chopped off your mountain, no one has touched a single wisp of your cloud or trampled on your sky. They've become two skies, two clouds, two mountains in your mirror whereas Helena who is languishing at the bottom of the ravine doesn't even have a pocket mirror to look at her bitterness right in the eyes.

Go away. Give that woman the time necessary to die a natural death and don't count on me to protect you if you insist on trying to restore the ruin. Being the mayor of a village of weirdos, drinkers of blood, doesn't give one the strength to put right side up that which has always been upside down.

Said the mayor.

Laure tossed and turned in her bed all night long and kept asking herself the same questions.

Why was Luc interested in the genetics of the Albanians of Malaterra when those of Castel Notta are better integrated and above all less eccentric?

Why didn't she wash and dress his body instead of leaving that task to the morgue attendant?

Why did she give his watch, the same brand and same shape as the Australian's, to charity instead of keeping it?

Why does the Australian insist on bringing dead stones back to life?

Why didn't she bring flowers to Helena when she went to visit her?

Why does the Kosovar sell old books that no one buys and not fruits and vegetables?

Why doesn't Postman Yussuf have a bicycle like all postmen worthy of the name?

And why didn't she bring something warm in her suitcase when the weather is turning colder and her departure from Malaterra is postponed every day?

The desperate cries of a blackbird scratch the window. Its flock gone south, it is languishing with a broken leg and a gaping wound on its side at the foot of the petrified tree. Laure, who had ventured into the crumbling house the day before should have put it up into its nest, but she lacked the energy to devote to a turmoil other than her own.

A lone bird, a lone tree, and a lone wall opposite her own solitude.

From Malaterra the Australian had retained only four exterior walls and eight interior ones. The weeks spent at sea had turned him into an amnesiac. He would have forgotten the name and address of his host without the paper his mother had slipped into his pocket as she shouted at him: 'Don't return before the blood of the girl on the soles of your shoes is dry.'

In return for his hospitality, his benefactor asked him to listen to him and if necessary to correct him; he had a great fear of forgetting the language of his country. Did words survive the Ottoman occupation and Communism?

He dug into the dry earth of his memory seeking the object and the word to describe it. His guest had only to nod or shake his head to approve or disapprove. From that confrontation between what the eye sees and what the voice says he deduced this: very few words survived their uprooting, two world wars. The words of the barefoot, the nomads, the travellers, assume the colour of the lands they traverse.

Néna imé, or 'mother' in Albanian became *mamma*; *nijé burré*, or man, became *uomo*; *nijé* or woman became *donna*; *falemindrit* became grace; *végéter* became old; *pranvera* became *primavera*. Only 'april' kept a bit of its origins: *april* unlocked the old man's jaws.

An immutable ritual, dinner quickly finished, the table cleared by a servant who was deaf and half-disabled, the old man pestered his guest. How do you say 'soul' in Albanian? And how do you describe it?

How might one respond when one has never encountered a soul or come across the slightest spirit? A cold sweat broke out of all his pores when the servant exited with the dirty dishes leaving them alone.

Sometimes Mikhaël de Durres would sing, at least that's what he thought he did, whereas he huffed and puffed the same hundred-year-old song about a red moon, a lock of blond hair cut and placed on the knees of the beloved. He became angry when the young man forgot to applaud. His fits of anger caused tempests in the sky, fed the anger of the elements, unleashed downpours, storms. His guest didn't defend himself when he called him a crook who had probably invented links of kinship to extract room and board from him, or even an assassin who probably had blood on his hands. He reproached him above all for having led astray their beautiful Albanian language with his journey and his inability to give him back the taste of things of his youth: the red berries picked from bushes, the water of the creek drunk in the hollow of his hand, his face turned to the sky, the poppy that calms the colic of infants and makes old people dozing in front of the fire believe a woman with milky skin awaits them in their beds.

Brief fits of anger like brushfire. His guest would flee, wander all night long, his neck bent under the rain. The storms ignited instincts of madness in his head. Unthinkable that a language could incite such passion. A language is like a poor man's soup, you throw in everything you have at hand. A language must die to be brought back to life, must be shared to multiply and grow, thought the one who shared nothing with anyone. No friends at all, his reflection in the mirrors he bevelled his only companion until he met Maria.

His hell, he said, came to an end with the discovery of an Albanian-English dictionary in a Syrian's bookshop. A big book half-eaten by mites. He learnt five words every day and spoke them to his benefactor who was amazed. Inversed overnight, their relationship went in an entirely different direction, he became the teacher and the old man the student. He snapped at him, called him lazy when his host pronounced a word badly or didn't answer quickly enough. The harsher he became the more his former tormentor admired him. The dictionary worthy of a trash bin avenged him of all indignities, all humiliations. His ascendency over Mikhaël de Durres became so great that the old man made him his only heir.

Mikhaël died soon afterwards. Slipped in between his hands joined in a pious gesture was the young man's precious dictionary.

'Who's Maria?'

Should she assume that the Australian's hand striking the air behind his shoulder is a response?

'Who is Maria?' Laure repeats.

Maria is the shape in red velvet with red hair on the jacket of a record, an elongated flame, whereas her hand on her throat is a cooling flow of wax. Maria, a voice listened to the way one stuffs oneself hoping to be disgusted by the food, his wife between two tours, married the way one throws oneself, head first, into a well. She wouldn't tolerate reproaches or recriminations; tears were allowed only on stage. She became bored in bed and forbade him from coming inside her since the birth of her son, born of her liaison with a baritone.

Absent for months without sending news, she got out of a taxi without offering any explanations.

'Here! I'm giving him to you. He is henceforth your son,' she told him, putting the baby in his arms before running to her room to unpack her suitcases.

Another pregnancy could have ruined her career—only caresses were permitted. She gave her milky body to his hands, to his lips.

Abandoned overnight, the frugality preached by the old mirror maker. Maria wanted everything all at once. The palace-like house, the orchestra that accompanied her when she sang, guests that had to applaud her. Busy playing Gatsby, he didn't see his impending ruin. The factory closed, hundreds of angry workers, he fled the way he had 30 years earlier. It was his destiny to flee. Only Bono came with him. Bono had raised his son. Bono the aborigine.

The mirror the only vestige of his life as a tycoon. It followed him in all his moves.

'Maria looked in it.' A weighty argument.

Was he delirious when he asserted that in it he had captured the image of his wife?

'She wasn't moving. As stiff as a dead woman. I am as much a widower as you, except you know where your dead husband is. I'm not so lucky.'

In the mood for confidences, both laughing and crying, he told her about the arrival in Sydney of his mother-in-law whom he thought was dead. Haughty, dismissive of all that wasn't Roman, the Italian *contessa* held her hand out to be kissed each time their paths crossed. She thought the way the house was decorated was vulgar, so she summoned a decorator from Milan who was mad for *One Thousand and One Nights*. Peacocks did cartwheels on the walls, lascivious women fanned themselves under the ceiling hung with pleated silk, a rutting ram flirted with a frightened virgin under a flowering almond tree. The artist painted and the *contessa* commented: the baobab is the tree from which her son-in-law descends, she explained to visitors, monkeys are his brothers, courtesans Albanian whores.

Humiliated at being dependant on him, she belittled him, called him a cuckold, a false Christian, a false father of a bastard, a nouveau poor after being a nouveau riche.

Strangely, the more she belittled him the more exhilarated he felt. A feeling of lightness close to ecstasy took hold of him as soon as she recited her rosary of humiliations. He levitated like Saint Anthony in the desert, deaf to the mouth that opened and closed without a sound coming out of it, smiled sweetly, held back his laughter. The *contessa* made up her hardships: her villa in Rome sold for a song in order to pay for her daughter's singing lessons, her jewellery pawned who knows why; memories as you know are the most beautiful inventions. Her daughter's marriage to this guy stuck in her craw. She didn't understand the choice, nor did he, it's as if the sun had married a locust. The Australian and his mother-in-law shared the same certainty and the same bottles of wine at the end of the day. The last bottle drained and their wobbly legs unable to take them upstairs, they fell asleep sitting up on the same sofa, the *contessa*'s head on her son-in-law's shoulder, and sometimes the other way around when the son-in-law wanted to change sides. Joined by the same fracturing absence of Maria who, a cold comfort, drowned them in press clippings relating her every move.

A concert in Milan followed by a weekend in Venice on the boat of a German industrialist, a concert in London and a weekend in the chateau of an English lord, cousin to the queen, a final concert in Beijing then three days in Macao, invited by the owner of several casinos. She called his complaining whining, his occasional calls childish stunts; the men who made him jealous were necessary for her to be known to a wide audience. Venice, Macao, London were professional trips. He was forced to believe her when he knew she was lying.

His wife was on another planet, and in a story that went far beyond his simple life. Both a diva and a kept woman. Ungraspable Maria. You might as well try to capture the light.

'There were three of us who suffered from her absence, except that the child who was asleep upstairs didn't know it.'

His wife, he said, confused the stage with life. No separation between the two. Back in her dressing room, the audience departed, she continued to consider herself Tosca and mourned the death of her lover.

Listening to him, Laure senses that the mirror behind his back is perspiring from shame.

The truck that dragged itself up the incline in a great din is filled to the brim. A miracle its axles didn't break, that it didn't fall into the ravine.

The aborigine and two workers unload sacks of cement, slabs of cinderblock and slag, floor tiles, bricks, a wheelbarrow, shovels and pitchforks, hammers, sledgehammers, rammer. The ceiling beams, the stone slab for the entrance will be delivered later with the front door and the cast iron balcony found in a second-hand shop. The Australian wants perfection for the house he was never able to mourn. The walls will be his determination sealed in stone, his childhood buried in the ground which will spread apart like a woman to receive the flow of cement necessary to strengthen the foundations undermined by wild plants and the infiltration of water from the melting snow.

The Australian's certainty is rock-solid, he looks defiantly at the ruin now that he possesses the weapons necessary to stand up to it, to be done with the sand and the gravel, and above all the petrified tree, a broom standing on its handle that has been taunting him since he returned.

He gives the order not to touch the exterior walls but to completely transform the interior. A half-circle platform facing the lawn on the slope is for the Steinway that will be delivered at the last moment.

'Maria can't live without her Steinway. Her voice and the sound of her piano blend in her throat, a flow of tenderness, river of despair, lava of hatred,' he exclaims in front of Laure who hears him talk about his wife for the second time in the same day. The first time this morning, in her house, coffee in hand, the second around his table unfolded by his valet for an improvised dinner.

Separated by the candelabra that flickers in the wind, he talks and she listens to him talk.

He doesn't eat and she watches him drink. He can't swallow anything until he has news of the singer. The doctor he consulted in Rome suspects a serious illness and has ordered a series of tests whereas his sickness is his wife. His illness' name is Maria. He will do more extensive tests when the construction is completed, when the diva moves in between his walls.

Laure, who can only agree, can see the house, the semi-circular platform, the anger of the December winds in the hallways, the snow that cracks the roof, even a fireplace that the master of the house hasn't mentioned, but not the woman with hair of fire, nor her cold hand on her throat that sings. Long when viewed from the side, curved when seen from the back, a piano suggests a boat and a casket. A closed lid won't reflect the face of the singer or that of the Australian who returned to this beloved but painful place. The mountain, he says, enters his chest when night falls, and prevents him from seeing the road that his wife will take to join him. He would level it off if he had the means to do so.

The construction is suspended, the two workers leave to have a drink at the cafe on the esplanade while the aborigine washes what he can in preparation for dinner. The earth seems to rise up, undulate, breathe when he sweeps up gravel and dust. Sometimes Bono cries, his tears falling vertically on his broom or on his hand when he leans his head to one side.

How do you say 'to cry' in the aboriginal language? wonders Laure who watches the cement dust that flies into the air, clings to the dwarf's thick hair, to his thick eyelashes, to the fur of the cats who become grey when they were once the colour of soot, then on her threshold, like ash from Pompei.

To the petrified tree that will be dug up tomorrow must be added a petrified man who won't admit it to himself, she says to herself, shivering with dread.

Harsh days marked by activity, transformed in the evening into convivial respites when his dust is gone, the Australian invites Laure to share his dinner and his anxiety.

Not overly friendly, nor surly, but disciplined, Bono who is no longer crying serves them, the same white napkin over his arm and the same expression on his face whether he is happy or tormented. Bono, according to his master, doesn't cry over himself but over the sun which dies every day at the same time. An aborigine ritual, a salute to his tribe over the continents and the seas.

The same gestures every night, the aborigine knocks three times on Laure's door and uses gestures to let her know his master awaits her for dinner. She accepts even though she has already eaten and follows him on the rocky path. The same opera aria greets her when she arrives. The soprano's voice rises up to heaven. Laure would believe in her presence without the record player in front of the mirror which reflects her voice and the darkness.

The glass of champagne, another ritual, raised to the voice that sings in the night, to the woman who never stopped rejecting and leaving him. Will leave him as many times as there are days in the year, and years in his life.

An old-fashioned staging. Whom does he wish to impress with this outdated ceremony? Why don't they put the platters on the tablecloth instead of making them go from one end of the table to the other? And why does the aborigine wear white gloves when his ancestors felled trees with their bare hands?

Seen through the weak flames of the candelabra, Laure's host never smiles, hardly touches his plate, but drinks. 'Stomach pain,' he explains, his finger pointing at his heart.

Yussuf doesn't want to bother her, doesn't want to intrude, Laure is busy with her new friends, Laure no longer has time to waste with a postman. The book he holds out to her through the doorway is a gift from the Kosovar.

The package unwrapped, she discovers a notebook and informs him.

'You'll make a book out of it,' he replies in a confident tone.

In his opinion, she has plenty of pencils and thoughts.

She just has to write down what she sees and hears beginning with herself.

Telling her own story will inevitably lead her to that of the Albanians whom she now knows like the back of her hand. When she gets to the postman, he'll assist her. Useless to ask advice from Helena who has a gun but no pencil or that of Mourad who uses books to light the fire of his oven.

Yussuf urges her to begin. The Kosovar won't be around very long. Everything points to it. He eats less quickly, speaks more softly, in shorter sentences and only in ancient Greek, a language according to him of a certain Charon who is soon going to carry him away in his boat to cross a river that no one here knows, even the teacher who is far from being an idiot has never heard of the Styx.

101

News of Helena? Of course he has some.

She wants you to know that she wasn't born yesterday, that the one you think is the Australian is not her daughter's rapist but a front man sent as a scout by the real guilty one to test the waters, find out if Helena still plans to kill him, he is waiting for her reaction to communicate it to his commander. But Helena who is far from blind has detected the deception. The difference between the black hair and the slender build of the coward who fled to Australia and the grey hair and thick body of the one who invites you to dinner is obvious.

'And don't tell me about age,' she shouted at those who snickered. 'The years don't turn a nightingale into an owl, or a quail into a frog.'

And she was on the verge of slapping them in spite of the whitlow on her finger, slapping the canary in its cage.

Helena goes further in her reasoning. She thinks that only the inhabitants of Malaterra who have a hard life stop looking like themselves as they get older whereas the years fine tune those who live elsewhere.

The one they call the Australian has a unique relationship with cement, plaster, and lines whether horizontal or vertical. Rumour has it that he intends to build a house large enough to invite all the inhabitants of the neighbouring village, but not big enough to invite those of Malaterra.

No useless movements, the man and his companion get straight to work, the workers clear the land of thorn bushes and gravel, they mix cement, transport it in a wheelbarrow, pour a slab of concrete before starting on the walls. No need for a plumb line or a T-square to be assured of their verticality, one need only look. Their work goes back to the first man who built the first wall to protect himself from wild animals and bad weather. The two men are humble in the face of what their hands, subjected to an order established thousands of years ago, are to accomplish. Joined by a thin layer of mortar, the stones piled on stones adhere together. Strikes of the chisel erase irregularities, adjust what is off, spatulas wipe off the smudges of saltpetre which in time will assume the colour of the stone. The dust raised by the wind covers with a thin transparent coating the hands that work. The Australian wants his house to be perfect: the flow of cement scraped off, unevenness smoothed by the spatula. The slightest carelessness seen as an offence to good taste. Invited to pitch in, chuckling observers offer their criticism.

'If I were him I would do this or that.'

'If I were him I would stop everything and go home.'

When the exterior is finished, the Australian will consult the doctor in Rome, though he has no need of a doctor to know what he is suffering from. His illness is called *sonnambula*.

'Mikhaël will take my place on the work site. He is my son since Maria gave him to me. He ended up looking like me from spending time with me watching for his mother's return.'

Has he forgotten that the one he calls his son has a baritone for a father and that the one he calls his wife is travelling the world on the arms of other men?

The postcards sent from Saint Petersburg, Kiev, Bucharest, Warsaw, Munich, pebbles strewn on her path. So many cities in so few weeks. Should he assume that her current lover is a travelling salesman, a sailor, an aeroplane pilot, a spy?

The few lines she scratches out say that she is travelling for pleasure, to take advantage of the last years of her youth, singing is no longer her priority. She has her entire life in front of her to sing. Then a final card, this one sent from Rome, which stuns the Australian. Maria demands an apology from the one who has nothing to apologize for before she will return to him. She promises to be magnanimous. To forgive him. She needs to be at peace, live a family life after so many years of restlessness.

'She must be desperate to return to me.'

The Australian says this, his eyes turned to a star, the only one visible at this hour of the night.

His painful laugh followed Laure to her bed, and continued ringing in her ears as she was falling asleep.

A prisoner of his laugh. He paid no attention to her when, thinking it might console him, she told him about Luc's absences and his return from Malaterra in a casket. Did he hear her? Filled to the brim with his sorrow, there is no room at all for anyone else. Nothing that occurs beyond his passion interests him.

No reaction, either, when she mentions Luc's work on the genetics of the Albanians and the difficulty of deciphering and rewriting his notes.

Only the word blood type brought him out of his stupor. His eyes lit up between two arms of the candelabra. The word blood stirred him. He uttered with a hate-filled voice the two words 'blood debt,' called them *rubbish*, and *savage*, and those who practised it poor earth scrapers, nettles stuck on their mountain.

Living in Australia, separated from them by hundreds of countries, he met them again in his nightmares, shouting, cruel, their eyes as sharp as the blade of a dagger. They envied our house built on a hill when they lived in huts dug out of the rock.

'A real house,' he stressed, and his arms in a broad movement raised invisible walls, connected by a roof.

'My father died when I was five years old, no one followed the casket. No one lifted up my mother who rolled her body down the slope, as custom dictated. Twenty times, thirty times in a row, brambles in her hair, her black dress torn by the pebbles. Lined up on either side of the steep path, the inhabitants of Malaterra watched the woman who rolled down like a barrel. Not a single hand reached out to help her up. It's a wonder they didn't applaud her efforts.'

Two unhappy people talk on either side of a table. The storm that is heard in the distance will not cross the mountain. The storm will turn back to more peaceful places.

'What if Maria refuses to move in here?'

A preposterous idea, Laure should have kept it in her mouth which had dried out from listening and saying nothing.

Her host's reaction: a searing murderous flash in his eyes.

A delegation led by the postman asks Laure to intervene with the Australian who is guilty of having sullied the reputation of the village. The rape which goes back three decades has cast shame on all its inhabitants. It makes sense that the Kosovar demands nothing, he's not one of them, neither Christian nor Albanian. Not from here. Must absolutely go back to his country.

There is war in his country.

'War doesn't frighten the nearly dead.'

'War frightens aeroplanes, not trains which go on running. You'd only have to squeeze him into a train car, he'll make the correct connections with the help of his Prophet.'

Basta talking about the Kosovar. They're here for the Australian. It's not to rebuild a few walls that he's returned to Malaterra, much less out of guilt for the death of Helena's daughter. Laure is assigned to interrogate him about his intentions, to convince him to compensate everyone even those whose daughters haven't been raped, even those who don't have a daughter. An injury inflicted on all. You are the spokesperson, you will be able to defend their cause in front of the rich man.

'Do you speak English?'

'One out of three words,' she admits.

'You say that word and he will guess the rest.'

The girl hanged from the fig tree continues to be exploited, everyone demanding his share of the torture she endured when none of them shared her terror, nor the pressure of the rope around her neck, nor her dying breaths and her wide-open eyes when all was over and her mother's cries alerted the neighbours.

Does she understand what is expected of her?

Laure nods her head.

They want her to be an accomplice to their monstrous blood debt. Ten coal-black eyes stare at her, follow her to the wall where she leans so she won't fall down. Is it the cold or laughter that makes her teeth chatter? The same effect for two different causes? Is she having a nervous breakdown to laugh and cry at the same time? Should they splash cold water on her, hit her head with a stick, gag her to stop that laughter, that chuckling, that sobbing?

Only the postman guesses the cause of her trembling. Laure is afraid, terribly afraid. The postman pushes the men with the coal-black eyes out of the room, closes the door behind them, has Laure lie down on the bed, massages the soles of her feet, her shoulders, puts a damp cloth on her feverish forehead. The things he mutters come from far away. They call upon the good spirits, the only ones capable of chasing away the malicious vapours. The postman recites a verse and Laure who trusts him no longer trembles.

The letter slipped under her door informs Laure of the departure of the Australian and of his request that she watch over his son who will take his place for the completion of the construction work.

Why is he giving her this responsibility when she is incapable of taking two steps in her room? A great fatigue has taken over her though none of the men with coal-black eyes has beaten or harmed her. None of them had a weapon or a stick. The men with coal-black eyes just looked at her. Indeed! A look sweeps a space without leaving an impact or a trace. A look doesn't leave an aching body. And how can she explain the bruises on her forearms when not one of them touched or even grazed her?

If she weren't so tired, Laure would go back home, the train station is a ten-minute walk, the train would take her to Paris where she has her apartment, not a room dug out of a mountain.

Less exhausted, Laure would ask Yussuf to stop keeping watch at her door, to put back in its sheath the dagger of his grandfather, a mercenary in the Ottoman army, and to go back home. Spending the night in front of a door isn't good at his age.

Thinking about it, the men with coal-black eyes didn't want her life, but her will, to impose her adherence to a belief that horrifies her: that blood debt that continues to pollute the minds of the Albanians of Abruzzo even when it is no longer practised in Albania.

A question haunts Laure: is there a connection between the visit of those men and the precipitous departure of the Australian, or should that be attributed to a cause other than fear?

When night falls, Laure is cold for the first time. August, which overheated the walls, has given way to the cool hands of September. In a few days those who live in the valley will rediscover their homes shut with huge padlocks and will face the wind that pulls painful rattling from the shutters. They will get underway after picking the last fruit, pulling up the last lettuce, and loading on their donkeys preserves, children, chickens, and jams. The old, women and children, will set off on the narrow path that leads to the mountain while the swallows migrate south, their feathers falling from their wings like snowflakes.

Her rifle on her shoulder, Helena will follow the movement after looking a final time at the fig tree. Should Laure believe Postman Yussuf when he says that after her daughter was put in the ground milk flowed from Helena's old breasts? A bountiful milk able to feed many infants but which no mother, even those with no milk, wanted. Did it come from Helena's dried up breasts or from the fig tree? Calling it the milk of blood, as if blood were a female that gave birth, the pale liquid having the acrid smell of wounds.

Blood: their ultimate reference.

Luc should have mixed their superstitions with their blood to better capture their DNA.

Enclosed within their consanguinity, they develop the same illnesses and the same resistance to certain viruses. Never tuberculosis, even though the droppings of pigeons filled with Koch's bacillus cover their roofs, their doorways. Never cancer, either, their cells don't allow the slightest drifting, but a great fragility of the kidneys, suggesting they nibble on the same pebbles and gravel as their chickens.

Postman Yussuf never tires of the story of the chicken and the prisoner stricken with the same depression. He would like Laure to tell it to him every day, even if he suspects that Luc made it up, put words down on paper for the pleasure of inventing and shocking. Only those who think get depressed, according to Yussuf. And so! The chicken that doesn't think can't be depressed. The chicken eats, sleeps, defecates, and lays eggs without thinking. With the knife at its throat it isn't aware that it is going to die. The chicken, a cretin, an imbecile, an idiot. With its comb removed, nothing remains. A tiny skull, and a chickpea for a brain.

Yussuf has answered his own question. Nothing to add, except that a depressed chicken stops laying whereas a depressed prisoner hangs himself in his cell.

They must come from far away to have such long legs and such
a big car, Yussuf says to himself, seeing the SUV stop in front of
the work site. A boy, a girl and a dog get out of the dusty vehicle.
They walk around the site, exchanging kisses at each stop, the
dog running around them barks to be noticed. The boy smooths
a pile of saltpetre with his hand, uses a stone to prop up the
mirror that looks like it's going to fall, makes sure the beam that
will support the roof is strong enough. Do they think they are
sheltered from the eyes of others when they take off their clothes
and lie down on the ground? The boy's mouth slides from her
neck to her breasts, nibbles on them one after the other. The girl's
moaning alerts the dog who joins the melee before being kicked
away. Two beautiful young bodies become one under the
stupefied gaze of the postman. He knows these things differently,
the man on top, the woman beneath. The continual reversal of
positions leaves him pensive. Postman Yussuf feels dizzy. Four
legs open, close, an indefatigable fan, knot together, unknot,
become tangled so that one can no longer know which leg
belongs to whom. Their panting is not a sign of fatigue but of
satisfaction due to the progress of the pleasure delayed on pur-
pose, the boy seeks a source as the proprietor of the place did
before him, digging in the ground sure of reaching the essential

water table. The constant movement ends with a throaty cry that fuses the two throats, he on top this time, she underneath to the great satisfaction of the postman, he falling onto her like a tree struck by lightning.

His head between his knees, Postman Yussuf is ashamed for them, coupling in nature like animals, without hiding, without holding in their cries, without muzzling their pleasure.

The scent of that pleasure, of the kisses, float in the air. Their laughter under the makeshift shower connected to the cistern brings Laure outside. She laughs along with them. She calls out to them and they wave at her through the curtain of water.

'Your father told me you were coming.'

'Are you Laure?'

Of course she is, she invites them to have tea and they dry off, put their jeans back on and rush over with their dog who is greeted by five furies who hiss their scorn in its face.

'The dog, outside! Be quiet, cats, and how many days do you plan to stay here?'

'As few as possible,' is the response trumpeted by two voices. Incomprehensible, the father's decision to settle in this godforsaken place, far from any city, to rebuild a house that he won't inhabit. His mother will never set foot in it.

To put back up the walls to bring Helena's daughter back to life, Laure thinks to herself.

With teacups in hand, they look at the walls around them. 'Amazing', 'My god' come out of their mouths swollen with love. Then that thundering 'wow' at the sight of a black spot on the ceiling. They decide together that what Laure calls a house must have sheltered the first man. Cro-Magnon or *Homo sapiens*? They hesitate.

'What did he eat?' asks the girl.

'Bones,' is the obvious response from the one she calls Mike.

Mike, like their Nikes the same colour as their jeans.

Sniffing the air with her little upturned nose, the girl says she can smell the bear. Her remark earns her a 'shut up, Sweet Rabbit'. But Sweet Rabbit continues and gestures.

Annoyed, Laure confirms, specifying that the bear moved across the way, to the work site. Disappears during the day, returns at night, devours anything that it finds, food or human beings, it's all the same.

Sweet Rabbit is panicked and decides to leave immediately to look for a hotel and Mike doesn't hold her back, nor does Laure, who doesn't like the Australian girl.

Leaning on the railing of the balcony above the valley, Mike says he knows about the dead girl and the blood debt demanded by the mother. Dad has told him everything. He asks her to find a solution. He, himself, is unable to.

'Your father should have talked to Helena himself.'

A suggestion greeted with a pained laugh.

His father, he says, has never dared confront reality. When a problem arises he invents another reality. He so wanted me to be his son that I ended up resembling him. Even ruined, he thinks he can reconstruct a ruin and offer the village a mirror factory to give work to those who don't have any. Month after month he puts off the ablation of his lung, convinced that the tumour is benign, and insists on considering my mother his wife, when she has changed lovers more often than co-stars on stage.

The day before his hospitalization, he took the train to the spa town where she was giving a concert and shouted his love for her through the closed door of her dressing room. Seeing that she wasn't opening the door, he offered a drink to the attendant, helped the mechanics carry the scenery, and asked the director, who was her lover, to watch over her. Satisfied with his excursion, he returned to Rome for his operation.

Would he have been another man married to a less unfaithful wife? Would I have been a different boy with a less eccentric mother?

Mike had been going to school when he was summoned home ostensibly just in time, his mother had convinced him that he would gain more knowledge by having contact with the extraordinary men she brought home. It was for his own good that she changed lovers, for his own good that she chose different nationalities, so he could learn languages without ruining his eyes reading books.

'All three of us believed her, but for different reasons. I out of laziness, Dad out of cowardice, and my grandmother out of racism. School for that Italian woman who claimed to be an aristocrat was a washing machine for the poor. One threw everything dirty into it. Crammed together on the same bench, Whites, Blacks, Yellows, Reds ended up bleeding onto each other. Close quarters were good for people of colour, she specified, but harmful to Catholic Whites. The aborigine sweeping the dead leaves in the garden almost gave her an apoplectic fit. She thought he was a giant spider then a monkey before crying out for help. The spider, the monkey? A diabolical scenario concocted by her son-in-law who wanted her dead knowing her repulsion at everything that didn't correspond to her conception of beauty, aesthetics, and normalcy. He's the one who put the monkey in the garden, he's the one who gave it a broom and orders to kick up the maximum of dust to suffocate her. Inside during the day, the longsuffering Bono henceforth worked at night when the Italian woman slept. The dust raised by his broom surrounding him completely, he looked like a zombie. The unearthed dead man continued to serve his masters.

Bono and Mike were the same height. The little five-year-old boy joined the aborigine in secret and shared his meals. Bono taught him to jump with his feet together like a kangaroo, to run backwards like a lizard. Bono's cubby hole was his school and Bono his teacher. The death of the grandmother sent back to Rome according to her wishes freed the aborigine who rediscovered the light of day.

'Not a single tear flowed from his eyes at the sight of the sun. An aborigine doesn't cry, and shows his bare buttocks more easily than his feelings.'

Says Mike.

Bono, who accompanied his master to Rome, is back, along with two workers. He will oversee the completion of the work. Mike will help him.

Any news of his master's health?

Excellent, he confirms even though his condition has deteriorated since the day before. A possibility that he'll die. If not, he'll stay at the hospital.

'Is he suffering?'

'Of course he's suffering, but he pretends he's not. A good way to trick death, ready to grab anyone who groans, when it flees like the plague the stoic who doesn't complain of anything.'

Proclaiming one is in good health, according to Bono, is the same as giving death a kick in the ass. Effective beliefs according to aboriginal statistics. The seriousness of the patient's condition doesn't play a role in his death or in his healing. They have seen dying people left to the vultures return home on foot, kiss their wife and offspring then gobble down an entire pot of beans and chili peppers because they had the right reflexes, transforming their last breath into a burst of laughter. Strengthened by Bono's lessons, his master smiled in his coma that morning. He would live long enough to see his house built, his wife settled between its walls, and to make peace with Helena. The last thing he said read on his lips:

'I will pay the *bissa* without discussing the price and will buy her a new rifle, hers is rusty.'

'Why a rifle?'

'To kill death' is the obvious response.

'You will kill death,' Luc had told Laure who asked him what she should do if he ever didn't return from Abruzzo.

'What if I can't?'

'Call the police.'

'Because the police are stronger than death?'

'Just as strong. The police are its main provider. They work hand in hand, collaborate to maintain order. Suppress demonstrations against hunger, unemployment, expelling foreigners, a godsend for the police who bring out their batons and revolvers, march with great strides, strike in every direction, blindly, without distinguishing between demonstrators and passers-by. Hit, shoot, drunk on the smell of blood, of that of the tear-gas bombs. The heavy boots stomp on everything that's on the ground, signs, those holding signs flattened under their soles before being taken to the hospital or the morgue or to the medical-legal examiner for an autopsy if there is any protest.'

Luc, getting heated, gesticulated. Did he think he was on a stage?

The last conversation. He was leaving for Abruzzo. The door closed behind him, Laure understood why her husband had chosen to study the Albanians of Malaterra. Their native Albania left behind for a stripped mountain, for a valley flooded three months of the year, they were subject to no authority, no dictatorship. Malaterra, a State inside a State, a blood type common to all, a pretext for Luc who wanted to re-join his brothers who refused to submit.

Laure senses her departure is imminent but doesn't know on which day exactly. Her suitcase is packed and Postman Yussuf is ready to take her to the station. He has even arranged for a wheelbarrow to transport all the Kosovar's books. While she was bidding him adieu the old man cried with a single eye, the left one, the right one laughed for who knows what reason. He, too, would be leaving soon. A train would take him to his native land with one chance out of a hundred that he would reach Pristina where battles between Serbs and Croatians were raging; stations were closed, connections cancelled at the last minute.

Laure looks from the books she will never read to the house that the Australian, in a deep coma, will not inhabit. His son awaits his death to go back to Australia.

Seen from afar, the house he'll inherit looks fine, walls standing, doors and windows reconstructed, only the roof is causing difficulties. The two workers dripping with sweat say the gods are against them. Someone from another world is preventing things from falling into place, from fitting together. Sitting on the walls, one foot dangling down, they forget to breathe when they see Sweet Rabbit who is soaking up the sun through all the pores of her naked body. The Australian girl is hoarding the heat before confronting the winter in Sydney and her job as a waitress in a cheerleader costume, with a rabbit's tail stuck in the crack of her bottom covered in black satin. Lying on a lounge chair, a thong her only article of clothing, she is unaware of the two men strangling on their saliva whenever she changes position, offering the spectacle of a blond armpit or that of a breast that flutters, a pigeon ready to take flight.

Sweet Rabbit and Mike took a walk yesterday on the square, hand in hand in leopard print outfits. The priest, the baker, and the habitues of the cafe thought they were terrorists. Frozen, the backgammon dice between their fingers, the extinguished hookahs, then great relief in discovering that the two eccentrics were the son of the Australian and his whore. Rumour had it they had sweet talked Postman Yussuf, promised him the moon if he went back to Sydney with them. *Basta* being the postman at his age, running around the streets with the dogs, knocking on doors to deliver nonexistent mail. Mike would buy him a real post office where he would be his own boss, with a table, a chair, stamping letters and sticking stamps that no longer needed to be licked.

Don't worry about the language, Mike assured him, breathing in the air of the country will be enough for you to speak English without an accent.

'Even the kangaroos speak English,' said Mike, and Postman Yussuf didn't say no.

Postman Yussuf trusts Mike who has already foreseen the venue, the former mirror warehouse in the middle of the jungle.

Postman Yussuf must absolutely change continents to change his destiny.

Arriving at Laure's door with the first ray of sun, Helena delivers a speech as long as the road that connects Malaterra to Rome. Laure is stunned.

'Helena,' she proclaims, is not a dog, is not a vulture. She will not kill a man in a coma. The proof of her good faith, she will give the rifle that was supposed to kill him to his bastard son, and will thus make him pay half-price the blood debt that has ruined her life. Helena cannot be bought, nor sold. It's out of the question to pocket the money of a cadaver or to sell a rifle that was passed down from father to father to her father going back as far as Cain who would have settled his problem of the firstborn with a bullet in the chest of his brother instead of strangling him with his hands. Helena has principles and a heart as big as the mountain, like her fig tree which feeds all the birds of Abruzzo. A true Albanian, Helena is capable of giving away her rifle, but not of selling it. Might as well sell your wife and children as that traitor Yussuf who emigrated to Australia did. The idiot told me about it, a smile on his face, forgetting my hatred for that country and for all those who live there.

'He suddenly showed up unannounced and accompanied by guess who? You'll never guess: by the rapist's son in person whom I thought was his own father from the resemblance, the same age, the same arrogant air, must take himself for the sun or for the streetlamp on the square to talk without looking at you, his eyes turned away. Talks while walking away. My rifle on my shoulder I would have torn him to shreds if the 30 years distance hadn't held back my finger. If the boy had died I would have turned the weapon on my own head before throwing it to the fig tree. Let the birds kill themselves off if they want, let there be none left to tell what happened.'

Her diatribe has exhausted Helena. She asks for a glass of water, drinks it down to the last drop, smacks her tongue on her palate.

'Where is Australia? Is Australia in America?'

'A bit lower,' Laure tells her, the same response she gave the postman the day she arrived in Malaterra.

'And why do the Albanians of Abruzzo all go to Australia when Italy is right next door?'

Laure forces herself not to laugh. Helena like all her country people is convinced that Malaterra is a small country in a large country. It's as if Italy were pregnant with Malaterra.

The end of the construction of the house coincided with that of its owner. The same day and same hour, when the workers left the site for good, their tools packed into their truck. The Australian died under the voice of *La Sonnambula* broadcast live from a festival in a spa town. The radio placed on his bedside table, the idea of a nurse taking care of him.

Nothing keeps Laure in Malaterra. She's going to go home, with the hope of finding Luc there, he who had accustomed her to his absences, Luc who would step impatiently through the entrance of their apartment will not allude to her absence, nor explain his own which lasted ten years. Laure will tell him about Helena, Ruhié, Milia, Fila, Yussuf, and all the others, but will keep to herself the Australian and his house with four walls on the outside and sixteen inside. Not a word about the strange owner and their agreement to make love to exorcise their hunger for Luc and Maria, without desire, without remorse, moved by a feeling of pity for themselves. They were Luc and Maria for the duration of a silent, stony coupling, their bodies like two statues. Laure opened herself to Luc and the Australian had entered Maria, to root her out, the breath of the singer and of the dead man filled the room; their names cried out in a pallid pleasure, painful before the abrupt separation when they realized they were only themselves. They were very cold afterwards. She was grateful when he left immediately, and he was grateful to her for not breaking the silence that filled the room.

Laure would above all tell Luc about the cats: having become big enough to take care of themselves, the lazy beasts ate from garbage bins, the bolder ones hunted. Their muzzles covered in bird feathers and egg yolks or exhaling fetid odours, the cats will coax a weak smile from Luc who stopped smiling on October 6, ten years ago.

What path did the Kosovar's letter take for it to reach Laure a
year after she returned to France?

My books and you gone from Malaterra, I had no one
left to talk to. The war between the Serbs and the
Croatians turned me into a suspect, the enemy of the
Christian Albanians. The mayor invoked the end of a
nonexistent lease to take back the shop. My armchair and
I on the street, they pushed us to the train station and
loaded us onto a train. Destination Pristina. A chaotic
journey. It changed its itinerary depending on the battles
that ignited cities and countries. Abandoned stations,
destinations cancelled at the very last minute. The one
and only traveller on board, the privileged spectator of
the destruction of a world. Stuck for a week in Ljubljana,
ten days between Zagreb and Banja Luka before another
interminable stop in Mostar. The bridge that divides the
city was uncrossable, desired by two peoples who
murdered each other on either side of the river. Now
we're heading to Żernica with the hope of reaching
Pristina by way of Sarajevo which has so far remained
neutral, but which will crumble under bombs as soon as

we arrive. Death around us, death as far as you could see. The train and I were safe. The bombs avoided hitting an old man sent back to his country.

Still alive the Kosovar who prays night and day to the god of locusts so that his army will devour the green and tender shoots of Malaterra, so that the door to the hell in the ravine will open wide to a horde of devils armed with pokers, that the priest dies choking on a host and that Helena's rusty rifle kills all the fig trees, all the birds of Abruzzo. What could be more terrible than a silent spring and trees without fruit?

Goodbye, dear Orpheus who did not find his Eurydice in the hell of Malaterra.

Ismaël